"It's

"What are you going to do, Princess? Why shouldn't I call your handlers and tell them I'm bringing you in?" Dylan asked.

At least he was willing to listen to her now. Honesty was her only hope. "I want to be free to have some fun. I don't know—take a walk, eat real food, play Frisbee. It's just one day out of my schedule. And I already figured out how the palace can respond to the media's questions. It's just one day...!"

Serena looked down in horror at her fingers. She hadn't noticed herself gripping the unrelenting muscles of Dylan's arm, hadn't known when she had pressed against him or when the pleading tone had crept into her voice. She uncurled her fingers, cleared her throat and murmured an apology.

He slipped a cell phone from the inside pocket of his jacket.

She felt a catch in her throat as he dialed. It was over.

"Yeah, it's me," he said into the receiver. "I haven't got her...yet."

Dear Reader,

When I was a little girl, I would sneak into my mother's closet and pull out her fanciest dress and heels. A little rummaging around her vanity drawer and I'd find the perfect shade of red for my lips. Then I'd open up her jewelry box. She had a choker necklace that gleamed like the Hope diamond times ten but which was probably just glass. I placed the necklace on my head, smiled winningly at the mirror and declared myself a princess. Never mind the dirt-smudged fingers, the ketchup stains on my T-shirt or my hair tugging out of its braids—I felt like royalty; therefore, I was royalty.

As an adult, I confess to being an avid reader of magazines and papers that claim to have the inside scoop on life as a royal. It's never as I imagined it as a child, but a girl can hope, can't she? At Harlequin American Romance, my editors have generously allowed me and you to have a little decadent fantasizing, to pretend that being a princess is exactly what it's supposed to be: adventurous, romantic, beautiful, with a tall, dark, handsome hero as the prince.

And that's what this book is all about.

I grew up to be a woman who still daydreams about being a princess. How about you?

My best,

Vivian Leiber

An Ordinary Day

VIVIAN LEIBER

Harlequin Books

TORONTO • NEW YORK • LONDON
AMSTERDAM • PARIS • SYDNEY • HAMBURG
STOCKHOLM • ATHENS • TOKYO • MILAN
MADRID • WARSAW • BUDAPEST • AUCKLAND

To Henry and Leigh Bienen

ISBN 0-373-16712-1

AN ORDINARY DAY

Prologue

"This is 'Entertainment Tonight,' reporting to you from New York City on what is rumored to be Princess Serena's last official visit to the United States on behalf of the monarchy. Her Royal Highness gave no hint of the turmoil in her country—or in her heart—as she arrived at Kennedy Airport this evening. Breaking away from her aides to talk to and accept flowers from well-wishers, the thirty-five-year-old princess, her divorce from Prince Franco a scant three weeks ago..."

"Shut that bloody thing off!" Sir Roger Cuthbert growled, his red jowls trembling.

The image of the blond, leggy royal flickered once, twice and then the eighteen-inch screen went dark.

Dylan MacPhail reclined on a club chair upholstered in a jet-black leather that exactly matched his jacket. He had made himself as comfortable as he wanted.

Five suits sat with Cuthbert at the conference table. Two others stood at the door, at attention, ready in case someone announced a surprise inspection of their glossy black polished shoes.

Dylan had been like that once. Fifteen years on Secret Service detail. Gray suits, white shirts, instantly forgettable ties. Hair cut to a precise one and one half inches. Posture rigid. Face expressionless. Eyes, with the potential to betray a man's soul, shuttered in smoky aviator frames.

Been there, done that, Dylan thought, resting a weathered cowboy boot on the glass cocktail table in front of him.

He wasn't Secret Service anymore.

He wasn't a suit...with good reason....

But a leather jacket, a comfortable pair of jeans, a cotton T-shirt and hair down to his shoulders hadn't changed the most essential thing about him.

He was good at what he did.

Some would say he was the best. And now he did it not for the love of his country but for the money, more money than he sometimes knew what to do with. His old pals, the ones who had stuck by him regardless, expressed a gee-whiz envy. He made his own hours, earned lots of money, mingled with celebrities as an equal and not a piece of furniture.

And no spit polishing those shoes.

Except the expressions of envy were meant to disguise the truth—his pals really offered up prayers of gratitude that they weren't him.

He did much the same work he had done all his

life. Protected his clients' lives, guarded their secrets, took the hits meant for them, and did it all so
matter-of-factly that the most goose-bump-ridden
client in the most dangerous situation felt something
almost like courage just from being around Dylan.
And Dylan had learned he liked his independence.

And he liked the money.

It couldn't make up for what he lost—but it sure
helped.

He wasn't surprised Sir Roger Cuthbert had
called. He was used to getting calls, his unlisted office phone number passed from one well-manicured
and bejeweled hand to another.

In the year and a half since he left the Service,
he had done security for the final concert for an
aging but still popular British superstar rock group.
The United States ambassador to the United Nations
privately hired him to accompany her as she toured
the battlefields of Central Africa. He had been called
in to negotiate the release of the kidnapped son of
a Washington D.C. millionaire. He saved the boy,
the money and even brought the kidnappers in to
the station house—all before the father could make
up his mind whether to bring law enforcement into
the picture.

Considering the jobs he had taken since becoming
his own boss, traipsing around the country after a
publicity-mad princess didn't seem like much of a
challenge.

And the money Cuthbert offered sounded good.

Very good.

Looking up from the table, Cuthbert caught his intense gaze and paled.

"I mean no disrespect to Her Royal Highness," the older gentleman said, ducking his head toward the blueprints spread out before him. "I just can't concentrate with the television on."

Yeah, right, Dylan thought.

The hotel room was part of the second largest suite in the Plaza. But the luxurious, five-star hotel room overlooking Central Park's lush greenery might as well have been a cheap roadside motel. The atmosphere was close, confining, stinking of bitter cigarettes and stale coffee. Worst of all, the plushly furnished rooms seethed with unspoken hostility.

Hostility directed at the beauty who was, at least for the moment, the most beloved royal of their country. Now ensconced in the most opulent and spacious suite of rooms directly above them, the penthouse suite of the New York Plaza Hotel.

"I'm still not clear on what you want me for," Dylan said. "You've got enough suits here to babysit her and you haven't mentioned any threats."

"There haven't been any threats," Cuthbert said. He made some pencil notations on the blueprints and his men studied his work carefully. "We have need for an American. We would like an American's perspective on things. And you are widely regarded as the best private agent available for hire in the States."

"Oh, really? And exactly what perspective do I, as an American, bring to this operation?"

Secret Service agents are trained to look. To see. To ferret out information with nothing more than a glance. Dylan looked at Cuthbert, whose face gave away more than most men in their profession.

"Americans are very innovative and, um, given to fresh ideas," Cuthbert said, jogging his square wire rims. "It's all that having a western frontier, I suppose. Pioneer mentality and all that."

Dylan uttered one word, one word only, said with a deadly calm that shocked Sir Cuthbert more than any shouted utterance could have. His lackeys at the table looked up sharply.

"Gentlemen, I will need a few moments alone with Mr. MacPhail."

Without protest or hesitation, the seven security men silently left the room. As the double hung tiger maple doors closed behind them, Sir Cuthbert hoisted himself from his chair and walked with steady dignity to the bar.

"Care for a whiskey?"

"No, thanks," Dylan said. "I'll be going now."

"Please don't."

"Then tell me the truth."

Sir Cuthbert sighed, poured himself a tumbler of whiskey and took the club chair across from Dylan. He allowed a small concession to his guest's casualness—he crossed his legs. Cuthbert was attempting to establish a personal rapport with him, but Dy-

Ian wasn't having any of that unless he knew why he was being hired.

Even if the money was good.

Maybe especially if the money was good.

"You wouldn't offer me this kind of money if there wasn't something special you wanted done," he said, rousing himself to call Cuthbert's bluff. "If you don't tell me what it is, I'm walking."

"Now, now, the reason I asked the others to leave is to tell you that there is something special about this job, but I need discretion. It is something that our country's agents cannot do given our constitution and our press, which has taken to emulating the American way."

Dylan had refused as many jobs as he had taken and this one sounded like a definite reject. Still, he was curious. The Princess Serena was a beautiful woman, if you went for drop-dead glamour, fresh-faced innocence and mile-long legs all wrapped in one package.

Which he did.

What kind of trouble was she in?

More important, what kind of trouble was she?

He leaned back and steepled his fingers.

"Now we're getting somewhere," he said coolly. "What exactly do you want from me? And be fore-warned, I don't kill for hire."

"Oh, no, nothing like that!" Cuthbert protested, waving away the odious suggestion with his pudgy hands. "We have a problem and we at the palace are convinced you alone can solve it."

"What's the problem?"

"Her Royal Highness," Cuthbert whispered, glancing about the room as if he expected "Hard Copy" and *Enquirer* reporters to be eavesdropping from behind the couch. "We think she has a lover."

"If that's supposed to shock me, I'm sorry. It didn't," Dylan said, purposely goading Cuthbert. The lord from the tiny northern European country wasn't playing straight, even with his conspiratorial whisper and practiced nonchalance. "She's still young, beautiful by any man's standards, and recently divorced. And let's not forget she's wealthy as all get-out. Why shouldn't she have a gentleman to escort her to all her functions?"

"Y-Yes, well," Cuthbert sputtered and Dylan knew he hit the good lord's weak spot. Rumors had been flying about the palace's displeasure with the financial settlement extracted by the princess's attorneys. "But, but, you understand, well, there still are issues of custody and succession which remain to be agreed upon. If the princess were seen as indiscreet..."

"With a little side action just like the prince?"

Dylan wouldn't ordinarily repeat anything he had read from a newspaper headline while in a grocery store checkout line, but the shock on Cuthbert's face was worth the crude reference to Franco's "longtime friend of the family," Lady Jane Howard.

"Mr. MacPhail, the princess is still constitutionally required to maintain her allegiance to the prince and to the throne," Cuthbert said impatiently. "Violating that allegiance, even by simply embarrassing him with an unwise alliance, is treason to the throne."

"Do you intend to behead her?"

"Certainly not!" uttered the horrified Cuthbert. "We haven't executed a queen under those circumstances in well over three hundred years."

"And you're not thinking of bringing back the old ways?"

"No. But an indiscretion could create a constitutional crisis of succession. Whether her sons Prince Erik and Prince Vlad will remain in line to the throne. And whether the divorce settlement has been made fair to the crown."

Dylan raised a weary hand. "And whether your Prince Franco can regain his popularity when he's sacked the fairy-tale princess in favor of the dear but dull Lady Jane?"

Cuthbert took a long pull on his drink and did not meet Dylan's eyes.

"So who's the lucky fellow?"

"We don't know," Cuthbert admitted. "She disappeared during the goodwill tour of India. She was gone for no more than four hours but we had to do some fancy footwork with the local officials to explain her absence. Last week, in Canada, she managed to elude her retinue for two hours, making her late for the ribbon cutting at the Ottawa General Hospital.''

''Did you ask her what she was doing?''

''She said she wanted to be alone.''

''So maybe she's telling the truth.''

Cuthbert gave him an oh-puh-leeze! look.

''She met someone. I'm utterly convinced of it.''

''So why don't you be more careful about following her? Isn't that what you bodyguards are for?''

''We are referred to as Lords of the Chamber,'' Cuthbert corrected. ''And no, they are not able to keep up, not when she really wants to get out from under them. Crafty little wench, I'll grant you that.''

Dylan arched his eyebrow.

''I—I meant to s-say,'' Cuthbert stammered, ''Her Royal Highness is a highly intelligent and very motivated young woman. Admirable really.''

''Smarter than your boys, huh?''

Cuthbert pressed his fleshy lips together. Dylan knew he shouldn't have enjoyed digging at the Lord of the Chamber but he did. He really did.

''Yes, unfortunately I must concede she's that. I need an outsider to keep tabs on her. I've considered the possibility that one reason she manages to escape is that one of the other men in the detail could be... Well, you yourself said the princess is a young and beautiful woman.''

''I see your problem.''

''Can we count on you?''

Cuthbert slid a color glossy eight-by-ten across

the cocktail table. It captured the princess as she accepted flowers from well-wishers outside a charity gala. Her pale gold hair was swept back from her porcelainlike face. She wore a white velvet gown that draped around her alabaster shoulders, a front slit highlighting her leggy frame. Her eyes sparkled like a deep blue ocean but were touched with a delicate sadness.

Blonde, blue-eyed, legs—she was exactly Dylan's type. The type that could tie him up in knots. Would he be immune to the charms that had captivated a country, if not the country's prince?

He looked up thoughtfully. "You know my record."

"Impeccable record."

Dylan allowed himself only the briefest moment to recall the bitter events that had changed his life.

A one-night stand that had cost him—everything.

"Some would differ. There was a little matter when I was on the detail covering the president."

"We know all about it. I meant, of course, that your record was impeccable and you were caught up in a situation not of your own making and…"

"I wasn't in the lady's bed against my will."

"You were the target of a partisan effort."

"I failed to protect the president."

"You were burned."

"No one forced me."

"Just between you and me—I think you were treated unfairly by the press and by your superiors,"

Cuthbert said, leaning forward, smelling of whiskey and peppermint. "I'm sure you'll never put yourself in that position again. And that's exactly what makes you a perfect candidate for this assignment. Because I can trust you won't. Ever. You absolutely won't be impaired by any attraction you may quite naturally feel for an admittedly beautiful woman."

"You're right. I won't."

Cuthbert swallowed the contents of his glass in a single gulp.

"I've always thought the American press made too much of that incident," Cuthbert concluded.

The two men stared at each other. Cuthbert looked away first.

For a scant second, Dylan thought he might like the man. Then the moment passed.

"I'll meet her," he said. "I'll work for you for exactly one day. Then I'll tell you whether I'll take the job."

And he promised himself if there was any doubt in his mind, any chemistry between them, any subtle sexual energy he felt, he would walk away. He still hadn't lived down the first time. There could be no second chance. Never again would he allow a woman to ruin him, however innocent or reckless the rules of attraction.

Chapter One

"The first scheduled stop in Cincinnati, Ohio, will start with brunch at the private residence of the president of the Covington University Hospital," Lady Bostwick said, scanning a fax transmitted by the palace. "Your host is Dr. Richard Speidel, who trained at Johns Hopkins and his wife's name is... Really, Your Royal Highness, with all due respect, you must pay attention."

Serena pulled the cashmere throw off her lap and stared out onto the tarmac of... It took her an instant's thought to remember this was Kennedy Airport, it was a half hour before dawn, and she was leaving New York for Ohio.

Fourteen cities in two weeks. Sixteen afternoon teas, seven intimate dinners with not less than a hundred guests, twelve ladies' lunches, eight formal balls, and every leftover minute crammed with tours of hospitals and schools, factories and galleries. Shaking hands with mayors, business executives, doctors, diplomats. All to raise money for her country's relief program and to generate much needed goodwill for her nation.

Even with almost two decades in the spotlight, she dreaded every minute of these trips, shook from nerves before each appearance, could not eat during the day if she was expected to give a speech at dinner and yet, she still shocked herself when she was declared a "triumph" at every turn.

The greatest public relations triumph her country had ever produced.

As she had been whisked by her staff from the Plaza rooms to the waiting limousine, she had noticed a newspaper headline already crowning her queen of the largest American city after just a day of appearances.

Now she was to take on Cincinnati. Was it the City of Brotherly Love, the City of Angels, the Breadbasket of America or the City with Big Shoulders? Was it the birthplace of Pete Rose or the hometown of Mickey Mantle? Did their team win the World Series? At the requisite press conference on the airport tarmac, should she make a joke about baseball, basketball, fair weather, foul weather, or the absence of weather altogether?

Lady Bostwick sniffed softly, her signature expression of displeasure. Following her lady-in-waiting's gaze to the cabin floor, Serena thought she recognized the source of her ire and quickly picked up the cashmere throw, folding it carefully over her knees.

If she got to wear her blue jeans instead of short-skirted designer day suits, she wouldn't get cold in the first place!

But Lady Bostwick's gaze remained fixed at a spot just beyond Serena's head.

Serena looked out onto the tarmac. Standing with the security detail on the tarmac, Sir Cuthbert directed last minute preparations for the royal jet. Next to him, partially shadowed by the rising whisper of predawn condensation, was a man Serena didn't recall as being part of the entourage handpicked by her ex-husband Prince Franco and his loyal Lord of the Chamber.

Wearing a weathered leather jacket and faded jeans, the stranger looked out of place in the circle of suits. Serena leaned forward to see better the dark curls that hung to his broad shoulders—a contrast to the crew cuts of the men on staff.

She wondered what was Cuthbert's business with this man, because Cuthbert was ordinarily quite derisive of men who didn't measure up to his stiff standards of formality in dress and manner.

And this man didn't look like he played by anybody's rules, dress code or protocol.

"Your Highness," Lady Bostwick prompted.

Serena glanced at her lady-in-waiting, whose pinched, magenta-colored lips parted in a barely there triumphant smile. And Lady Bostwick never smiled.

Serena slipped the shade down over the window. "You may go now."

A half century of training in deference to royals forced Lady Bostwick to her feet. But she lingered over the folder of information prepared for the Cincinnati leg of their trip.

"Your Highness, this information is vitally important and I think it behooves you to..."

"The president of the University Hospital's name is Richard Speidel," Serena interrupted, staring Lady Bostwick directly in the eyes. "His wife's name is Liz. Their two sons, David and Andrew, attend private schools out East. They have a dog named Sparky and an aquarium of unnamed goldfish. They collect eighteenth century Dutch Realism paintings and nineteenth century pendulum clocks. And, by the way, the Covington University hospital is actually across the river from Cincinnati in Covington, Kentucky. It's not actually part of Ohio."

"Very good, Your Highness," Lady Bostwick said, bobbing a briskly defiant curtsy. She reached for the folder lying on the tray table in front of the princess. Serena grabbed first.

"I will study this myself," she said.

And she would.

By the time the royal jet touched down, Serena would have memorized the names and personal histories of every guest at the morning's brunch. And the specialties of each of the doctors and nurses she would meet on the tour of the cancer unit at the

University's hospital. And she would have something special to say to each of the luminaries she would greet in the receiving line before dinner at the Cincinnati Arts Council.

She was motivated by terror. Pure, wake up in the middle of the night trembling kind of terror. Worse than any Halloween chain saw multiple-murder scary movie playing on her hotel television set. She was terrified of failing her country, of causing embarrassment, of playing into the stereotype of her country's stubborn disdain for anything created or anyone born later than the twelfth century. She was a representative of her country, a determined good-will ambassador, a tireless advocate of investment in her country's greatest resource—its people.

For them, she was terrified of letting them down.

She was even afraid that her divorce might have caused some hardship to her people.

And that hurt, far worse than the actual pain of knowing that she had failed at marriage, far worse than the loneliness of her separation. She vowed that she would do anything to make it up to her countrymen. And to her sons, who were being groomed to become her country's leaders.

And the palace had suggested a course of action that the topmost aides had described as doing just that—making up for a failed marriage.

The only price was her freedom.

"Lady Bostwick," she said, softening her tone. After all, they were both devoted to one goal—their country's health and well-being. "Lady Bostwick, I need some time to review the materials before we touch down. Some private time."

"Very good, Your Highness."

As Lady Bostwick closed the cabin door behind her, Serena threw her cashmere throw right back onto the floor and stretched her stockinged feet. She opened the folder and stared at the first page of the palace report.

When a knock came at the door she murmured a "come in" but did not look up when the cabin door opened to admit Lord Cuthbert, who was recognizable simply by the smell of the peppermints he favored. Out of the corner of her eye, she noted Cuthbert's well-polished oxblood wing tips.

And then she saw the black cowboy boots next to them, and her eyes moved upward to the slim denim-covered hips. A woman would have to be comatose not to respond to the way the soft fabric hugged every muscle, tightened at every curve.

A woman would have to be comatose...or a princess. A very determinedly chaste princess, which she was. She could never, ever allow a scandal.

She spared only a cursory glance at the stranger's broad chest, wide jaw and lazy grin, and then the Royal Highness returned her attention to Cuthbert. Who was looking rather smug.

"Yes, Cuthbert?"

"This is Dylan MacPhail, Your Highness," he

said, bowing from the waist. "He will be helping out with security."

She noted a muted disdain in the American's blue-gray eyes that made her wonder if Cuthbert had been filling his head with stories about her.

But she also saw a bluntly masculine appraisal.

He wasn't playing it cool.

He wasn't playing it starstruck.

He wasn't playing it anything at all.

He looked at her as a woman, seeming to struggle with some kind of conclusion about her.

She picked up the cashmere throw, wondering if she was cold, afraid or merely modest.

Although that last thought was ridiculous since she was wearing an impeccably proper pastel peach suit.

But the American had awakened something in her, something Lady Bostwick must have sensed before she herself did. How else to describe her lady-in-waiting's Cheshire cat smile?

Serena narrowed her eyes, pursed her lips tightly, and returned to her study of the facts that would help her get through the Cincinnati stop.

"I thought we had adequate security arrangements," she stated.

"But, of course, Your Highness," said Cuthbert with his trademark oily tone.

"Has there been any change in the political or economic status of our country?"

"No, Your Highness."

"Have there been any threats against me or the throne?"

"No, Your Highness."

"Any of our security detail taking a sudden leave?"

"No, Your Highness."

She looked up sharply. Did they know what she planned to do when they reached Chicago, their final stop? Is that why they needed this American?

"Have you discussed this with His Royal Highness?"

"We haven't informed him specifically that Mr. MacPhail has agreed to join us, no, ma'am," Cuthbert said, digging into his pocket for his mints. "But, Your Highness, I assure you, Mr. MacPhail will be an asset. He has a definite American perspective we think could be helpful."

"And what precisely is the American perspective?"

"It's unique," the American said, shooting an amused glance at Cuthbert. "It comes from having a Western frontier."

"You're kidding me, right?"

"No, Your Highness," Cuthbert chimed in. "Americans are very...unique. Pioneer spirit and all."

"Oh, really?"

Serena dared to look directly at the American.

"What are your qualifications as a unique American?"

"Secret Service. Fifteen years," he answered flatly.

She shook her head. "You don't look Secret Service."

He reached into the inside pocket of his jacket and held out two cuff links with the presidential seal. The ones that the president of the United States gave at his discretion to faithful friends and family.

"Well, your colleagues don't grow their hair that long," she observed.

"I also don't wear a suit." He shrugged, putting the cuff links away. "I don't have to follow Secret Service guidelines anymore."

"The long hair looks good. Too strong of a jaw for short hair." Cuthbert said. He looked up from his peppermint tin. His eyes met hers. "And the casual clothes really fit him better than any suit could, don't you agree, Your Highness?"

She glanced again at the American. He didn't look happy having others discuss his physical attributes as if he were a beefcake model.

"I hadn't noticed his looks one way or another," Serena said curtly.

Cuthbert looked up at the American with an expression she recognized well. See what I have to put up with? he communicated.

"Good day, Mr. MacPhail," she said, and realized that an American would not know that he was expected to bow to her. American men never bowed.

But even a man born on the North American continent had to know when he was being dismissed.

She willed herself not to look up when Cuthbert bent ever so slightly and hustled the American out. She looked up only as she heard the cabin door click shut. What was Cuthbert up to?

The pilot announced that the jet had been cleared for takeoff and asked that the staff and the princess fasten their seat belts. As they briskly taxied onto the runway, Serena pulled up her shade and stared at the approaching dawn.

New York's day was just beginning, with millions of women just like her, readying for work, waking their children, kissing the men in their lives good morning. Serena would do anything for a chance to trade her life for any of theirs.

But her selfish thoughts were stopped dead by the competing claims of her two sons and a country.

Quickly calculating the time back in her country's time zone, she buzzed the captain and asked for a telephone line to be cleared.

"I'll have that for you as soon as we reach cruising altitude, Your Highness," the captain said.

"Thank you," Serena replied. She leaned back in her seat and smiled as she anticipated the phone call. Nothing could take this away from her, she thought. And then she frowned, thinking of the American. She could make no missteps before Chicago.

"SHE'S BEAUTIFUL, isn't she?" Cuthbert said, as he yanked his seat belt around his girth.

"I suppose," Dylan conceded.

"So, can we count you in?"

"I told you I needed a day."

"What do you need more time for? You've met her. You've seen the layout of the plane. I gave you the itinerary. We've already got the cashier's check prepared. All you have to do is say yes."

"Yeah, but I need to decide."

"Decide what?"

"Just how beautiful she is," Dylan said grimly.

Sensing that he shouldn't say another word on the matter, Cuthbert snapped the black polyester mask over his eyes and announced he would take a quick nap.

Chapter Two

After she concluded her phone call to her sons, Serena pulled open the folder of information about Cincinnati and stared for several minutes at the guest list. But the names weren't coming together, her normally fine-tuned concentration was shot and she knew herself well enough to guess the reason why.

She also knew what she had to do.

She thought things through carefully. Dylan MacPhail was handsome as the devil, and she was a princess. He had a wicked grin and knowing eyes. She was vulnerable. He was an American, unused to the distant formality royalty extended to commoners.

She was attracted to him.

It was a perilous situation.

She couldn't dismiss him outright—Cuthbert and Bostwick would guess her motivations immediately. And would spot and exploit her weakness to their advantage.

Serena couldn't offer him money—her money

was more tightly controlled than when she was married. A hunk of change given to an American in exchange for him leaving the security detail would be a nightmare to explain.

But she couldn't allow him to continue as a part of her entourage. She would reveal herself and her attraction, with a word or a glance—and the admission of feelings would cost her.

As she saw it, she had only one weapon at her disposal.

She looked down at the plate of scrambled egg whites and grapefruit slices the cook had sent from the back cabin. Promising herself that she would make it up to the chef some other time, she buzzed for Lady Bostwick.

"Yes, Your Highness?"

"I want this breakfast taken away. The eggs are too…runny. Have the cook prepare another plate."

"Yes, Your Highness."

She sent back the next breakfast with the complaint that the eggs were too stiff. The third breakfast she sent back, sniffing that the eggs were too…eggy.

"I want a firmer pillow," she said to Lady Bostwick.

"Yes, Your Highness."

Minutes later, she buzzed her lady-in-waiting again. "No, a softer pillow. This one is too firm."

"Yes, Your Highness."

"By the way, tell Cuthbert the temperature in the front cabin is too warm. Do something about it."

"Yes, Your Highness."

Minutes later, she called Cuthbert to her cabin and told him she was too cold.

His oxenlike resignation to her demands made her falter. He was acting most unusually...cooperative.

But two minutes of reverie about the way the American's jeans fit, and she jammed the buzzer hard.

"Cuthbert, the temperature is too warm again."

"Yes, Your Highness."

"And tell Lady Bostwick I want the book I was reading last night."

"Yes, Your Highness."

"And a cup of tea. Make sure it's not too hot. And not too cold."

"Yes, Your Highness."

When she figured she had everyone in the back cabin roused to a fever pitch of loathing, she called for her trunk to be brought up. The staff crowded in the cabin doorway, and she felt, rather than saw, the American's disdain as he slouched against the doorjamb.

"I wish to pick out different shoes," she said to Bostwick. "Ones that better match this suit."

"Yes, Your Highness."

With Cuthbert and Bostwick staring openmouthed, she dumped the contents of her Louis Vuitton shoe trunk onto the carpet.

"I can't find what I'm looking for," she declared, nearly losing her nerve. She reached to put the shoes away but she turned on the American.

She couldn't falter. She had to act decisively. This was not the time for second thoughts or hesitations.

"Here! You there. Put these away."

He shook his head, his face betraying neither distaste nor anxiety. Two emotions she had hoped to engender.

"I don't do shoes," he said.

"Cuthbert, order him immediately to—"

"Your Highness, he's an American. I can't order him to do anything."

"He's part of your security detail."

"Only for one day," MacPhail said.

"Why only one day?"

"I have to decide whether I like the job."

He looked at her with a dead-on challenge.

She gritted her teeth. She'd make this American hate her. He'd leave. She'd be safe from making a fool out of herself because of her nagging vulnerability.

She shot a glance at Cuthbert.

"He can stay if he chooses," Cuthbert said. "He said he'd decide at the end of the day."

"Then your first duty and perhaps your last duty in your short tenure here, Mr. MacPhail, is to take care of these shoes," she ordered, tilting her chin regally. "Alphabetical order by color."

She had gone too far. She could see that in the blaze of lightning-quick anger that coursed across his features. In the way his blue-gray eyes flashed like burning opals. In the way his jaw muscles rippled like a racing thoroughbred's thighs.

Perhaps he would jam his fist against the wall, and then he could be dismissed immediately as being a loose cannon. Maybe he'd insult her or throw something or swing a punch at Cuthbert. Maybe he'd swear. Or refuse to do her bidding. Or quit right here on the spot.

Then it would be over.

But he did none of these.

Instead, he knelt down, never taking his eyes from hers, silently commanding her to look at him, and then he picked up a purple peau de soie pump.

Damn. Double damn. He was going to stay.

"I'll be in the other cabin," she announced.

"Oh, Princess, just one last thing," he said amiably. "Before you go—do you think I should consider this shoe as *E* for *eggplant* or *P* for *purple* or *L* for *lilac* or...?"

She growled an unintelligible reply and escaped from the cabin.

"YOU SEE WHAT we have to deal with?" Cuthbert asked, popping a mint into his mouth. "The rest of the world has no idea. Want one?" He held out the open candy tin to Dylan.

"No, thanks," Dylan said, barely taking his eyes from the princess. She had changed into an ice blue sleeveless dress with matching pumps and a wide-brimmed straw boater.

Three hours late for a brunch. A half hour circling in the air space above Cincinnati because the princess wouldn't get off the phone. Two and a half hours spent trailing behind her as she shook hands and accepted flowers from the welcoming crowd that seemed to get bigger with each passing minute.

"She's nothing like what the public thinks," Cuthbert continued. "But most of the rich and famous aren't, wouldn't you say?"

Dylan nodded noncommittally.

"But it's like that joke about elephants," Cuthbert said. "Where does the princess sit?"

"I have no clue."

"Anywhere she wants." Cuthbert chuckled. "Get it? Anywhere she wants?"

Dylan shrugged. Cuthbert's sense of humor escaped him. Maybe it was from living in a country where people didn't vote.

"I know it's a little early to ask, but will you be staying on, Mr. MacPhail?"

Dylan watched the princess hand off a bouquet of lilies to her lady-in-waiting. The flowers she had already accepted filled the back of the security limousine and would be donated to the Covington University Hospital.

She was beautiful, no doubt about it. Even more so than her pictures suggested.

She sure knew how to work the crowd, stopping

to chat with anyone who wanted to talk. And they all wanted to talk to her, to be the focus of her smile, if only for a moment.

Cuthbert was right—the public had no idea.

He didn't have any illusions. He watched Cuthbert's team and regarded them as professionals. They could protect the princess competently enough. Dylan wasn't being hired for protection—she had plenty of that. He was being hired just as Cuthbert had declared. To tail her. To discover her secrets. To find the mystery lover. To nail her for her indiscretions.

Everyone, even someone as uninterested in foreign royals as Dylan, knew the story of the princess. A fairy-tale romance when she was just eighteen. A prince who had avoided marriage for so long that the rumor mongers declared he was, well...but the rumors were forgotten in the maddening delight of the royal wedding. The requisite heir was born exactly ten months after the nuptials, and the spare produced a scant year and a half after that.

And then, a profound chill. That deepened as the princess grew in confidence and stature. Her popularity among her own people and around the world eclipsing her husband's. A few years ago came a privately arranged separation. A terse announcement from the palace.

And now, the very public divorce.

Through it all, the prince denounced as a cad. His romance with Lady Howard uncovered. The princess regarded very much as a heroine, a victim, a martyr. Her wistful smile tearing at the hearts of her fans. When she socked a photographer who came too close as she cried on the day her divorce was granted, she was applauded.

Dylan wasn't buying it. Not after today.

The princess was a royal...witch, he concluded, tempering his opinion only slightly. But he was glad she was. Because beauty didn't mean a thing if it came packaged in a sour disposition. She'd be hell to work with. But a job was a job. The money was good, though it didn't make up for losing everything. But it was better than nothing.

He held out his hand to Cuthbert, suppressing the uncomfortableness he felt as his firm flesh met the squishy fingers of his new boss.

"I'd be honored to come on board," Dylan said. "You can count on me."

THE TELEPHONE woke him, two short and then one long shrill ring. Dylan pulled his head out of his pillow, lifting his wrist to check the time.

What city? He riffled through his choices.

Cleveland, Detroit, St. Louis, Indianapolis, Nashville...

Sweet Home Chicago, he concluded, after a quick study of the hotel stationery.

Rrriiinnnggg!

What could the royal witch want now, he wondered.

It was six o'clock in the morning, a scant three hours since the princess had been escorted by the staff at the close of the Field Museum ball. There had been an hour in the hotel manager's office, cataloging the jewelry which had adorned the princess's beauty and which now would be safely locked away until the next evening. Serena had taken forever to admire each piece—the tiara, the earrings, the necklace, the bracelets....

Dylan could have wrung her neck, he just wanted to get some sleep.

The princess had closed the door to her room at five, peau de soie heels in hand—pearl, not gray, she snippily informed her entourage. Her beige Fortuny pleated silk dress had looked a little wilted. Her French twist had pulled apart into soft, golden waves.

She had looked bed-ready and more beautiful than ever.

But Dylan had felt not the slightest desire to touch those curls or caress her bare leg. He wouldn't have kissed her if she had asked, wouldn't have made love to her if she begged.

But in his dream...damn her.

He grabbed the phone.

"Yeah?" he barked.

"Cuthbert here. We have a situation."

"What is it now? Her pillow too soft? Or too hard? Or too pillowy?"

"She's gone."

Dylan was wide-awake.

"I'll be ready in five."

"We're in her rooms."

Dylan jerked himself off the bed, yanking off the tux he had been too tired to take off an hour before. He grabbed a pair of jeans, ran a comb through his hair, threw water on his face and decided it would take too long to shave the shadow from his chin.

In the bedroom, he loaded his gun, shoved it in his shoulder holster and put his leather jacket over it. He had a license to carry, but he didn't like to advertise. And he didn't know what to expect.

He took the fire escape stairs two at a time and found the window of the princess's suite of rooms open. Lady Bostwick was sobbing into her handkerchief and three of Cuthbert's men circled the sitting room, either looking for evidence to help them find a princess or simply dazed that she had eluded them.

"Lady Bostwick, gentlemen, sit down," Cuthbert said, getting off the phone. "I know your feelings run high."

"The spoiled little…" Lady Bostwick's face paled as she searched for the right word. "The spoiled little…tramp."

The room suddenly fell into shocked, sullen quiet. Dylan slipped into a chair at the door. He leaned back, balancing the chair on its back legs. He crossed his arms over his chest, feeling the reassuring scrape of the gun against his chest.

"Now, now, Lady Bostwick," Cuthbert chastised. "Regardless of our personal feelings, we must remember that the princess is a member of our royal family and the mother of two heirs to the throne." He tilted his head toward Dylan. "This is precisely the situation we hired you for. How long will it take you to find her and bring her in?"

"I have no idea what she's up to or where she is," Dylan said. "But Chicago's my hometown. If she's anywhere in the city, I'll nail her faster than I would have anywhere else. When do you want her and where?"

Cuthbert glanced at Lady Bostwick. "The luncheon given by the mayor's wife at eleven," she sniffed, adding indignantly. "The princess wanted the whole morning off."

Dylan bit back the observation that the princess had come back from the ball not a minute before nor after her scheduled departure. She had to sleep sometime.

He told Cuthbert he'd like to search the other rooms of the suite.

"My men have already done that."

"I want to do it my way."

Dylan wandered through the rooms, smelling the lingering, expensive scent of rose and jasmine the princess favored. He paused at her bed, untouched from its turndown, the folds still ironed into the glossy white coronation lace trim of the sheets she insisted on traveling with. A slip of paper peeked out from under the pillowcase. Embossed with her royal crest.

He returned to the sitting room.

"Serena's presence should raise so much money for our country," Lady Bostwick hissed at Cuthbert. "It's an opportunity not to be missed. And after the luncheon is the tour of the restored church and the tea given by our consul general. To say nothing of the reception this evening. She must attend these."

Cuthbert raise his hand.

"Lady Bostwick, I have hired Mr. MacPhail and I trust him. He will find her in time for the luncheon. She will be brought to heel."

"I don't know about that," Dylan said, strolling out of the princess's inner chamber. He held up the piece of ivory bond notepaper. Cuthbert snatched it.

"Damn her," he muttered. He read the note aloud. "The princess is regrettably indisposed with the flu, her appearances canceled until Friday."

"Heavens!" Lady Bostwick cried.

"Totally unacceptable," Cuthbert said.

Dylan slipped the note from Cuthbert's fingers. He memorized the scent, the loopy scrawl, the ink spot at the bottom of the page. If she had a lover, it shouldn't be any of his business. Or these people's, for that matter. And he should feel sorry for the man who had to put up with her. But he had been paid. And she had signed on as a princess.

"I'll be going now," he said, heading for the door.

"Are you going to find the princess?" Lady Bostwick cried. "She must attend that luncheon."

"When can you get the princess back?" Cuthbert demanded.

"I'll let you know," Dylan replied over his shoulder. "Relax. This is what you hired me for. I'm bringing her in."

As the door slammed shut, Lady Bostwick shot a pleading look at Cuthbert. "Oh, dear, have we done the right thing?" she whispered.

Cuthbert smiled maliciously.

"My Lady, I am positive we've made a most excellent choice."

Chapter Three

Serena looked at the full-page color photograph of herself on the cover of the morning's *Chicago Tribune*. Coming out of the private residence of Northwestern University's president the previous afternoon, she was dressed in the ecru Gucci suit with a matching bag and spectator sling backs. University President Henry Bienen stood at her side, beaming to reporters.

"Excuse me." A businessman jostled her, pulling the topmost *Tribune* out of the stack. He threw a couple of coins on the dirty wood counter of the kiosk.

Serena looked at the remaining *Tribunes*. Had to be at least fifty papers, but the owner of the kiosk on the busy Lincoln Park neighborhood corner did a brisk business in the early morning. He dispensed newspapers, gruff hellos to regular customers, and paper cups of hot, acidic-smelling coffee.

She looked again at the paper, fascinated by the image.

Wow!

The one-word headline was used to describe herself.

It still surprised her to see herself in photographs or video feed. She felt she bore little resemblance to the glamorous woman dressed in up-to-the-minute haute couture and the smooth, cultured voice delivering sound bites sounded foreign to her ears.

Did she really talk like that?

As a teen growing up in a back country estate, she had been shy and gawky. Her laugh had been more of a giggle and too quick in coming. She thought preparing for dinner involved nothing more than changing out of her jeans, always muddy from the bracing country rides on her favorite horse. Her hair was as often as not pulled back with a rubber band into a simple ponytail. Sometimes she chopped it off in front of the mirror when she became impatient with its wild waves. Her nails had been short and stubby, her face sun toasted.

She had been a tomboy, through and through.

In the course of the ''romance of the century,'' the palace had sent a legion of specialists to her parents' farm. Cosmeticians, dietitians, fashion designers, manicurists, dance teachers and an elocution expert who taught her to speak in a throaty, cultured voice. Even a riding instructor who taught her the formal English-style mount and forbade the bareback riding she grew up with.

By the time she was presented to the world as a

bride, she was a poised and polished beauty. She had set fashion trends for nearly twenty years, bringing about the fad for wheat gold blondes, sharply tailored suits and pink champagne lipstick.

She was an ornament, really. Wonderful to look at, too fragile to hold and completely useless. At least, that's how she had come to feel about herself.

But she had never given up her jeans, though they fit just a little snug after two children and many years. And she had never forgotten how to cut her own hair—though she had not done so in years.

"Hey, lady, you gonna buy the paper or what?"

She startled at the gruff voice, unused to strangers speaking to her—and without even using her title!

"Cough up the fifty cents, lady. Or beat it. This ain't the public library."

The kiosk owner leaned over the counter, his ruddy face scrunched into a menacing frown. Serena looked down again at the picture of herself, taken just the day before. Did she look anything like...?

"She's very pretty," Serena said with an American accent, pointing to the picture.

"Yeah, yeah, she's a beautiful angel," the owner conceded, his features softening. He looked up sharply, as if expecting a scam. "But that don't change the facts. It's fifty cents for the paper. Or you gotta move on."

Serena dug into her pocket. Royals don't carry money—that's what Lady Bostwick was for—and Serena hadn't wanted to attract suspicion by asking for any. So she had only a few coins and bills that she had squirreled away. And little of it in American currency.

Fifty cents was a lot of cash—funny when her divorce settlement was widely regarded as one of the most generous in the world. Still, she was so pleased that the kiosk owner didn't recognize her that she happily counted out four dimes and two nickels in American money. And then, after wishing him a good morning, she continued on her way.

"Hey!" he yelled after her.

"What?"

"You forgot the paper you just bought."

He held up the newspaper, glancing at the front page and then at her face. Serena stood rooted to the spot, so afraid she felt like a little child about to be scolded. The owner did a double take and then held out the paper to her.

"You know, you could be as pretty as a princess, too, if you tried a little makeup and maybe let your hair grow out a bit."

Serena reached up to touch the wispy strands of her pixie-short hair. The rest of her hair lay at the bottom of the wastebasket in her room at the Drake hotel.

"Yeah, maybe I could look like her," she agreed, taking the paper. "I'll keep that in mind."

Serena threw the paper in the trash when she was out of sight of the kiosk. She ordinarily read three papers each morning—the *Wall Street Journal*, the

London Times, and the official journal from her own
country. Contrary to reports from so-called insiders,
she didn't scan the papers for articles and pictures
of herself. She generally skipped the gossip pages
and zeroed in on economic and political news. She
had gotten into the habit when she had thought she
could feel more comfortable at state gatherings if
she was well-informed.

It hadn't worked—people in power seldom expected or wanted her to do more than smile
sweetly—but the habit of keeping up with current
events had stuck.

Now she had twenty-four hours before her life
was effectively over. Skipping the papers one morning could be forgiven.

She checked the street signs—Webster and
Clark—and headed north. She was meticulous in her
preparation for goodwill trips, so Lady Bostwick had
not quibbled when she had asked that a Chicago
street map and a tourism directory be included in
her preparation file. Serena headed North on Clark,
passing the site of the St. Valentine's Day massacre,
and marveling at the architecture of the former gov-
ernor's town house.

No one recognized her. Sure, a few men turned
as she passed—a second glance, nothing more. She
was as anonymous as the city. Her euphoria was
nearly uncontainable. She had planned this day
nearly to the minute and it looked as if it were going
well.

First she wanted a cup of American coffee at a typical American diner. But as she beelined past a trendy java joint, she felt a sudden prickling at her neck. She turned around, scanning the street.

Nothing.

People heading for work, people waiting for the bus, people walking their children to school.

But she had spent her adult life being tailed by discreet, barely noticeable security. She knew when they were there, knew when she was being followed.

Palace security or dogged paparazzi, tough to say which would be worse for her.

Quickening her steps, she cut down a side street that would lead her to the Lincoln Park Zoo. She prayed her recollection of the map was correct.

She looked back once, nearly tripping as she saw him.

He was big.

He was fast.

And he was gaining on her.

The American had apparently been hired for more than his good looks and ability to annoy and arouse her.

She broke into a run, crossing the narrow formal gardens that surrounded the Lincoln Park Conservatory. The fragrant blooms of geranium, pansies and impatiens drooped with dewdrops. Dirty gray pigeons scrambled out of her way. A man pushing a grocery cart piled high with his possessions yelled at her to slow down.

"Hey, Princess!" The American shouted.

She bolted through the loading zone where school children on field trips were lining up for tours of the zoo. Serena remembered the brochure—on Wednesdays, the gates opened early. She ran straight through the open archway. She passed the seal tank and the reptile house and then realized she was all turned around.

There was a parking lot around here somewhere and if she could just get to it, she would know how to get to the lake....

"Your Highness!"

She darted past a group of teenagers with backpacks, knocking over a young boy. With a shouted apology, she darted onto the open shoreline of the Lincoln Park Lagoon.

But she was no match for him, and as she heard his gathering stride behind her, she saw her future diminish and darken to a black dot even though the brilliant sun had just climbed up over the sparkling clear turquoise water of Lake Michigan.

It couldn't end like this—not after she had planned so carefully!

But she knew her defeat even before he tackled her to the dewy grass. His leather jacket swooped over her like the wings of a predatory eagle.

Knowing rationally that she had no choices, no options, no chance of getting out from under him—but still unwilling to surrender—she fought. Hard. With everything she had. Kicking at him, but finding no purchase. Clawing, and ruing her decision to clip her finely kept nails. Squirming out from under him only to have him bring her down again.

It wasn't enough.

"Hey, you! Whoa! Stop it!" he shouted. He seemed as surprised by her fight as she was. He subdued but did not strike back. He grunted when she managed an awkward but true kick to his stomach—but he didn't retaliate.

"Let...go...of...me!"

"What the hell's the matter with you, Princess?"

She screamed and cried, now unable to stop the tears even though scant minutes before she would have claimed that she would rather die than have the American see her so debased. But everything—a whole lifetime of memories yet to be made from this one day—had been taken from her.

He pinned her arms down on the grass and sat astride her. The ease with which he brought his will to bear upon her made it clear that he could have overpowered her, could have outrun her, whenever and however he chose.

Only now did he think it worthwhile to do so.

That fact depressed her even more than if she had narrowly lost her battle.

"I asked you—what's your problem?"

"I won't go back!"

"You have to go back! They're waiting on you at the hotel."

"I left them a note. They should just say I'm sick. Even princesses get sick."

"Yeah, well, you just got well. I'm taking you in myself."

"I won't go!" She grunted through gritted teeth, fighting though she knew that when he tired of this cat-and-mouse struggle, he would drag her in. She had no recourse against his strength.

And it was pointless to argue.

Equally pointless to explain.

Americans couldn't understand the subtleties of royal succession, of obedience to the throne, of loyalty to the crown—or a princess in a forever prison of her own making.

"Are they physically hurting you? 'Cause short of that, I don't see why I shouldn't take you in."

"No, of course not. They're not allowed to even shake hands with me," she said, dismissing the notion promptly. "But I'm still not going back. It's worse than physical. I just can't go back. I just can't go back. I just can't go back."

As she defeatedly moaned her sorry mantra, he lifted one hand. For an instant, she feared he might strike her. But there was such tenderness in his eyes, some softening that she hadn't noticed in him before.

He touched the hair at her forehead, damp with sweat, smelling of salt and baby shampoo. She felt her tears return anew, but now she cried for the gentleness in him. The gentleness that she knew was not to be repeated for her. Ever.

So long since she had had any kind of physical contact at all—that must explain the heightening senses.

"That's a helluva haircut," he said gruffly. "I always liked long hair, but I guess this is kinda cute. And I'll betcha women all over the world are going to be chopping off their hair by nightfall."

His words soothed her, even if the content was inane. His finger, coarse with calluses, moved on to touch her cheek, to brush away the tears. He looked at his wet fingertip as if discovering only now the nature of sadness.

"What's wrong, Princess? How come you don't want to go back? You know I gotta take you in, unless there's a good reason not to. Now I know you don't like me, and I'll be honest, I don't like you. But you gotta trust somebody sometime and it might as well be me. Right here. Right now."

She could tell him.

She could tell him everything, lay everything out, try to get him to understand, and then swear him to secrecy. But then she would have to expose herself to him. In a way that no tabloid or official portrait or exclusive interview had ever done.

Out of the corner of her eye, she noticed two uniformed police officers approaching. They were still fifty feet away, but they were clearly observing though they munched on doughnuts and sipped coffee as if they were on break. She knew watchful when she saw it.

Serena thought of how she must look to them. A tear-stained woman beneath a much larger man. One of his hands pinning down hers above her head.

Later she'd think it through and decide it was a terrible idea, but she did the first thing she thought might work.

Chapter Four

She screamed.

Ignoring the look of shock and then betrayal that crossed Dylan MacPhail's features. Ignoring the way his free hand curled into a fist and then dropped limply to the grass beside her face.

"All right, all right, what's the problem here?"

The two police officers yanked the American to his feet, cuffs holding his arms taut against his back.

Even restrained, she sensed that if he had wanted to shrug them off, he could have.

But he didn't.

He was a big, strong man with a chiseled face—the scar on his forehead looked as if it might have come in a fight and he looked as if he had a lot of struggle left in him.

She was five-eight, only a few inches shorter than he, but where he was full-bodied and hard, she was fine-boned and rail thin.

And she used their differences to her advantage.

"He overpowered me," she said, rapidly improvising. "He's crazy. He was following me and he tackled me down to the ground and he wouldn't let me..."

She hadn't said anything that wasn't true, but she sure hadn't explained everything. And she didn't want to. She waited for the American to jump in, but he didn't.

Just stared sullenly, his blue-gray eyes hooded, his jaws rippling with suppressed emotion.

"Do you know this guy?" The officer at Dylan's back asked her.

"Yeah, he's... We've known each other for about a week. And I just wanted some time alone and he wants to take me back..."

The officers barely let her continue before they jumped in with their own conclusions.

"Okay, man, settle down. Take a deep breath. Sometimes you gotta be cool with women," said one of the cops, carefully placing himself in between Serena and the American. His name tag identified him as Kerner. "Now just take another deep breath and think about what you're doing with her. She's your woman, right? You're a good man and you wanna treat your woman right. Don't you agree?"

"I'm not..."

Click!

The older officer jerked the handcuffs tightly on his wrists. Dylan winced but said nothing. It wasn't pain that coursed silently across his features, but an anger at the loss of freedom.

He was being trussed up like an animal and she instantly regretted what she had done.

"Please let him go! I shouldn't have screamed. I just wanted to get out from under him. I wanted him to leave me alone."

Officer Kerner shot a knowing glance at his partner.

"They always say that," the partner said. "They always back off, afraid and all."

"No, you don't understand," Serena exclaimed. "I wasn't in my right mind. I just didn't want him to take me back to the hotel. I didn't mean to get him into any kind of trouble!"

"Princess, start running," Dylan urged softly. "Get out of here. Now."

She couldn't see his face, hung low with his dark hair covering his eyes.

"Stop talking to her. She's not going anywhere," the older cop said. "Miss, we're going to want to take a statement from you."

"Princess, get out of here," Dylan repeated.

"Don't say a word, buddy," the older cop ordered, yanking the handcuffs tighter. "No more intimidating the lady."

"I think we should bring him into the station house," Officer Kerner said. "Why don't you come with us, ma'am? You can file a report. We have some counselors who can talk to you about this kind of thing. You know, domestic abuse and getting out of a codependent relationship like this one."

As he tugged at her sleeve, Serena came to her senses.

"Domestic abuse?" she asked.

"Yeah, we don't want you to feel scared any longer. Come on to the station house."

Come with them to the station house? No, absolutely not!

She hadn't considered they might want to hang on to her.

"No," she said. "I'm sorry, I can't."

"Run, Princess, run," Dylan said.

She saw the officers' mouths open to big, round Os as she took off, running as fast and as hard as she could back through the zoo. She didn't trust herself to look back until she was far away. Winded, she doubled back to the conservatory building and then she had to shell out a dollar to look at tropical plants just so that she could stay out of sight.

She sat down on a wrought iron bench under a banana tree and willed herself not to replay the bare moment of tenderness the American had shown her. When he had touched her hair, her tears, when he had told her to clear out, to take off. He hadn't been protecting himself, he'd been watching out for her.

She was sure that protective impulse would disappear when he was thrown into a jail cell. She wondered if he would get out of jail before she got up the courage to walk back to the hotel.

This was going to be difficult to explain to Cuthbert.

Worse to explain to the palace.

"WE GOT NO complaining witness now, but don't think for a moment that I won't remember your face," the older officer said, shoving his chin up against Dylan's. "Next time there's a report on you, fella, I'll be there. If there is a next time, your girl will file that report. Now let's see some ID."

Bob Kerner unlocked the cuffs. Dylan slowly brought his hands around to his front, rubbed the red of his wrists and reached into the inside pocket of his jacket.

"Careful now," the older cop warned. "Don't make any sudden moves."

Without disturbing his shoulder holster, Dylan brought out his wallet and flipped it back to his driver's license. The older officer looked at it twice, studied Dylan's face, and then opened his mouth in frank surprise.

"You're MacPhail?"

"Yeah. What's it to you?"

"You were handling security for that British rock group, whatever their name was. You donated fifty tickets to our precinct's D.A.R.E. project last time they were in town. Made a lot of the teens happy. I thank the Lord and my precinct captain I didn't have to chaperon that unruly crowd."

Officer Kerner peered over the shoulder of his partner, checked out the ID and looked up at Dylan.

"What are you doing slapping around your girl?

Don't you know you can work these things out without resorting to violence?''

"I wasn't..." Dylan stopped short his denial. If he explained everything, the princess was ruined. Utterly ruined. And though she had betrayed him just now, he knew he was her only defender.

Though he called Chicago home, he had no illusions. It was a tough town out there, with dangers she wasn't even aware of. He had to get her. Now.

"I wasn't thinking," he concluded with a heavy sigh. "I wasn't thinking straight and I promise it won't happen again. Can we keep this incident between ourselves?"

"Sure, we have to. We don't have the lady no more," said the older cop. "But I don't want to hear about you being involved in this kind of stuff again. Get some counseling, man."

"Yeah, how can you do this?" Kerner chimed in. "You're Charlotte's brother, aren't you?"

"How do you know her?"

"I work with her," Kerner said. "And how would it make you feel if some guy was slapping her around?"

"I wasn't... Aw, I give up."

"That's good, that's good. Admitting a problem is the first step toward a cure," the older cop intoned.

Dylan endured another five minutes of lecturing on domestic violence, particularly ironic since he had never raised his hand in anger against a woman, child or pet.

And the only men he had ever fought with had asked for it.

But he kept his mouth shut until he sensed the officers were finished with him. Then he made a courteous goodbye and sauntered off with seeming casualness. He made sure not to follow the dainty footprints on the grass, faintly outlined with dewdrops. The two cops were still watching him.

Instead, he headed toward the lake.

He would swing around and pick up her trail.

He'd find her.

He just wasn't sure what he'd do with her when he did.

TWENTY MINUTES. Twenty minutes of her life stuck in a conservatory next to a banana plant. Well, actually a rubber plant, from Indonesia, according to the placard that she had read out of boredom a halfdozen times.

She was at war with herself. If she stayed on the bench, she could see anyone coming into the conservatory or leaving the conservatory. She'd see the police and she was sure there would be police. Sooner or later, Dylan would have to come clean about who she was. All he had given her was some lead time.

To scream had been a stupid, impulsive thing to do—she had been dreaming of her freedom, her one day of freedom, for so long that reason had flown right out the window.

Lord Cuthbert and Lady Bostwick were probably in heaven right now, with the titillating scandal of a runaway princess about to break. The palace would be called, and no doubt the carefully crafted deal she had made to protect herself and her sons and to do right by her country would be destroyed.

Just the thought of the crush of reporters and photographers and cameramen and gawkers as she returned in humiliation to her privileged prison—it was too much to bear.

The day of freedom she had planned for so long was gone, forever gone. Conceding that, she figured the best thing to do was probably to go back to the hotel—and beg. Beg for mercy that would no doubt be denied.

At exactly twenty-two minutes after she had run away from the police, she walked into the bright Chicago sunlight. The air was warm and moist. The flowers laid out on the conservatory grounds fluttered in the light breeze, showing off their brilliant red, yellow and pink blooms.

Her heart went *thaddump* when she saw him.

He was eating a hot dog on the park bench, as nonchalant as if he were a man of leisure. He looked right at her.

He'd been waiting.

She walked over, knowing she wasn't going anywhere he didn't want her to.

His eyes narrowed. He took a final bite of his hot dog and wiped his fingers with a paper napkin.

"Don't ever do that to me again," he warned quietly. "Now, sit down and explain. Everything."

She stood completely still. She looked to the left out of the corner of her eye. Looked to the right. The path to Lincoln Avenue. The other way went right to the lake.

"Don't even think about running," he said.

"What if I screamed again?" she asked. "The police might not be so quick to let you out of their hands this time."

He shook his head.

"You won't scream. You're a princess on the run, you don't want Cuthbert and Bostwick throwing a fit and the tabloids would have a field day destroying your goody-two-shoes image. You're lucky I didn't turn you in."

She flinched at the last, but squared her shoulders regally. She wasn't quite defeated. She still had the two weapons that always worked. The first was a straightforward command. "I'm not going back," she said. "And I'm ordering you to return to the hotel. Alone."

"Sorry, Highness, I take my bodyguard duties very seriously."

He was bigger than she, even more so when she wasn't wearing her heels. She felt intimidated by his height, by his confidence and strength, but most of all by his total disregard for her station in life.

Still, she had spent her adult life as a princess. And she wasn't about to be sidetracked.

"You're fired."

"You didn't hire me."

Why am I not surprised he doesn't respond to commands? she thought. It was time to bring out weapon number two. Money.

"Then I'll hire you. Double whatever Cuthbert offered you. Make that triple. And then I'm ordering you to return to the hotel."

Dark indignation swept across his face.

"A deal's a deal," he said coldly. "I don't break my word. I can't be bought out of a promise. Cuthbert and Bostwick said to bring you in."

"And you'll do it?"

"Yeah, I will. You've got a lunch with the mayor's wife in three hours and at the rate it takes you to get dolled up, you'll still be several hours late. Even with the new haircut."

"But I can't go back!" she wailed.

"Then you'd better explain everything to me," he offered mercilessly. "Otherwise, I'm taking you in. And no funny stuff this time."

"Funny stuff?"

"Screaming. You know, you're pretty naive about how the world works. I could have toasted your reputation just by telling the cops who you were. And you would have brought it all down on yourself."

"Thank you for not saying anything," she conceded, head down.

"If that's an apology, I'll take it. And now I want answers. Otherwise..."

She looked up into his hard-as-steel eyes, knowing he'd throw her over one shoulder and stride back to the Drake Hotel without breaking a sweat if she didn't talk.

And he wouldn't be stopped by any royal protocol.

Chapter Five

"All right, truce," she said, slumping onto the bench.

"Good job, Princess," he said, reaching around to clap her shoulder as if she were his oldest friend. "I knew we'd come to understand each other. Now, do you want a hot dog before or after you tell me your tale of woe?"

She looked doubtfully at the hot dog nestled in waxed paper. It was slathered with mustard, relish, ketchup, sauerkraut, onions, hot peppers and would have ordinarily been quite disgusting this early in the morning.

"You eat it with your fingers," he instructed, with what she considered entirely too much cheerfulness. "Oh, yes, I forgot. There is this." He held out a paper napkin.

It had been years since she had eaten anything that wasn't served on Wedgwood, with a sterling silver fork or spoon.

But if she had only a few more moments of freedom, she might as well grab what pleasures she could. Besides, she hadn't gotten breakfast.

She took the hot dog and snapped up the napkin. Maybe just one bite. Sort of an experiment in the real American cuisine. Not the stuff of five-star restaurants.

He watched her eat, her bites getting larger and more enthusiastic. She yanked open the accompanying package of chips, scattering crumbs for the voracious pigeons who cooed and billowed at her feet.

"That was great," she said, minutes later, after washing down the last of her hot dog with a cold can of soda.

He gave her another napkin. "Now it's payback time," he said. "What? Certainly you didn't think the hot dog was for free. You start talking, filling me in on what I'm missing."

She shook her head. The food had given her some fight back.

"I'm not telling you anything. Yet. First I want to know why you were hired by Cuthbert."

"Bodyguard duties."

"No way. You might be good. You might even be the best. But I've got plenty of guards—and in fact, I dare say the palace wouldn't be at all unhappy if one of the guards were a little remiss and I took a bullet or got run over by a car. It would be a tidy solution to my ex-husband's public relations problems. In fact, maybe you're just the man for—"

"I don't do contract killings."

"Then you won't mind telling me the real reason Cuthbert wanted you."

"Haven't you been listening to him? I have a unique American perspective on things."

The look she gave him communicated exactly what she thought of his "unique American perspective."

"I'm not talking until you start talking," she added primly, pressing her advantage.

"All right, I suppose it doesn't matter if you know. They think you have a secret lover whom you're meeting. They want me to find him and you. Hopefully in an incriminating situation."

"*I* have a...*lover?*"

"Sure. Why not? Some men would say you're quite a dish."

"Thanks for the compliment, but—"

"You're wealthy and available—"

"Thank you, but—"

"Still, you're spoiled and flighty and spend more time getting gussied up than any woman I've ever—"

"Thanks for that unique American compliment, but I still can't figure out—"

"I mean, I wouldn't want to be your lover because I like women who are nice. But—"

"Thank you!" she said from behind gritted teeth. "I can do without your pitiful editorial comment. I just want to know how I would ever manage to have a secret lover? Contrary to what the press reports, my palace aides know exactly where I am every minute of the day. They would know if I had a lover—they wouldn't need you to tell them. Even with your 'unique American perspective.'"

"There was India."

She glanced quickly at him, wondering how much Cuthbert had told him.

"Sure there was India. I wanted to walk through the Taj Mahal. I put on the veil and the conservative Bengal sari. I was blissfully on my own. No reporters, no crowds, no dignitaries to make forced small talk with. No bodyguards, either. Completely anonymous...and completely chaste."

She didn't tell him that the temple dedicated to romantic love had made her so aware of the hollowness of her own life that she had come back from her hours of freedom in tears.

Tears that she hid from her staff by claiming a migraine and demanding—with seeming petulance—total isolation in her room.

Now she knew exactly how those hours of freedom must have appeared to Cuthbert and Lady Bostwick. She should have hid her feelings better.

"And then there was Canada."

"Canada was the same thing," she said. "But I went to a movie."

"Which one?"

"Which one what?"

"Which movie?"

"I...I don't remember. It was something with Jean-Claude Van Damme."

"There are a lot of Van Damme movies."

"This one had fighting."

"They all have fighting."

"He was the hero."

"He's always the hero." He glared at her. "Who is he?"

"Who is who?"

"The lover."

"There isn't a lover."

"Look, people act unwisely when they're in love or they think they're in love or they just have something as simple as lust. And a lot of people ruin their lives with chasing after this thing called love. And they take other people down with them."

"You don't need to give me a sermon about ruining my life. I know enough about the subject to teach you a few lessons."

"I'll bet you do."

He looked away sharply. She thought he might have seen something or someone. Perhaps he had been followed by one of Cuthbert's men. Perhaps she had been.

But tracking his gaze netted only the sight of zoo keepers cleaning the elephant cage. He was offended. And she couldn't afford that.

"You can tell Cuthbert there is no lover," she said. "And there won't ever be. You tell him I understand the terms of the deal quite well and I intend to live up to my side of the bargain so long as the palace lives up to its part.''

''What deal?''

''The deal I made with the palace upon my divorce,'' she explained. ''After this trip, I'm to take residence in the palace on the Isle of Whit.''

''Isle of What?''

''Whit. It's a remote archipelago up near the Arctic Circle. It's our northernmost territorial possession. There's a twelfth-century castle there that once housed a convent. Can't get to it except by helicopter and when the winter winds come up, you can't get in or out at all for several months at a time.''

''How long will you stay there?''

''The rest of my life,'' she said.

''The rest of your life? No way.''

''It's the absolute truth that I'm going. My next stop after Chicago is my last.'' Here she allowed herself a touch of pique. ''No goodwill tours that upstage my husband. No gala balls where my dress or my hairdo can be compared too favorably to my ex-husband's lover's. No sympathetic interviews with the press, no candid photographs, and certainly no romances to spark the public imagination. Not even an occasional escort.''

''Will that helicopter you talk about get you out for little jaunts?''

''No, the only time I will leave the castle, if ever, will be for my eldest son's coronation.''

She saw at once that he was a man who valued

his freedom. And was suspicious of any woman who would give up hers.

"And this is what you did to get all those millions?"

She looked up at the heavens and counted to ten. And then an extra ten for good measure.

"I agreed to this because I want to ensure that my sons maintain their rightful succession to the throne and I wanted to help my country pull together after the crisis of my divorce."

His eyes narrowed. "Have you talked to your sons about this?"

"No, of course not. They don't know anything about the deal. I told them I was tired of public life. And the palace would never tell them otherwise."

"And do they want to succeed your ex-husband on the throne?"

"I...I don't know. We've never discussed that."

"Then how do you know they want this prince thing bad enough that they'd be willing to trade having their mother be in a prison—a very nice prison, but still a prison—for the rest of her life?"

Serena grumbled impatiently. This was the problem with talking with commoners—they were dogged in their questions, utterly without self-consciousness in asking for every detail. In fact, this exact situation must be the sort that the originators of royal protocol were thinking of when they made up the rules.

"They don't have a choice. They're princes.

That's what they are. That's what they are born to. Just like I was born to a noble family from which my ex-husband had to choose his wife. I simply made the mistake of thinking we were in love.''

She immediately wished she hadn't admitted to that last. Though true, and certainly the subject of speculation in the press, she was ordinarily quite private about her feelings. But Dylan didn't seem to notice the emotional nuance. Or maybe he was too much of a gentleman to comment. She figured he hadn't noticed. The alternative was clearly wrong.

"How old are your sons?"

"Seventeen and fifteen."

"Don't you think they're old enough to choose? To be anything they want to be—princes, cowboys, doctors, construction workers?"

"No, they're still children."

"When do you think a man becomes a man?"

It was a reasonable question to ask, and yet the way he said the words made her flush. He must have noticed her discomfort, for he quickly added, "When I was your older son's age, my father died and I took a job to help support my mother and two sisters. My mother probably didn't want me to work, but she knew she couldn't stop me and she needed the help."

"I don't want or need my sons to sacrifice anything on my behalf," Serena said, tilting her chin proudly. "I have accepted the deal from my ex-husband. And I will honor its terms."

She didn't add that the breakdown of the marriage had so destroyed her self-confidence that she had not fought the terms laid down by the palace at all. She had nearly, in her grief, welcomed the exile in some small way.

"So why are you running off now?" Dylan asked.

"I want freedom. Just one day of freedom. To have a memory to carry with me for the rest of my life."

"What are you going to do? Assuming I don't drag you bodily to the hotel right now."

She sensed an important resistance in him had been overcome. Perhaps he would see things her way, would understand her needs, would let her have just...just twenty-four hours. She hardly dared look at him, certain she would be reduced to begging.

"I want to do the things that normal women do."

He bit his upper lip absently. "What kind of...um...things do you have in mind?"

"Oh, God, nothing like that," she said sharply, immediately understanding his sexual nuance—making love to a man, a real man, was too ridiculous to even fantasize about.

Besides, what she'd experienced in making love had persuaded her that while sex was obviously necessary for the continuation of the species, it wasn't worth all the love songs, romantic movies and best-selling novels.

It certainly wasn't worth raising Cuthbert's ire.

"I just want to... I don't know—take a walk, eat real food, play Frisbee, go dancing."

"Dancing?" He raked a hand through a disobedient lock of hair. "Princess, I've been with you for almost two weeks, and you've gone out dancing just about every night."

"Without a ball gown."

"And for this you're going to stand up the mayor's wife, blow off the tour of the restored church, and no-show the consul general's tea?"

"Guilty as charged," she said. "But I thought of all this. It's the last days of the last tour. All Cuthbert has to do is put out the story that I'm sick with the flu and our Chicago hosts will be happy to reschedule for the day I should have traveled back. It's just one day, one day out of a schedule..."

She looked down in horror at her fingers. She hadn't noticed herself gripping the unrelenting muscles of his arm, hadn't known when she had pressed against him or when the pleading tone had crept into her voice. She uncurled her fingers, cleared her throat and murmured an apology.

"Who is he?"

"Who is who?"

"Your man. The one who met you in India. And Canada. And are set to meet here."

"There isn't any man," she snapped.

He slipped a cell phone from the inside pocket of his jacket.

She felt a catch in her throat. "Who are you calling?"

"Cuthbert."

As he dialed, she cursed herself for her weakness and wondered if she should make a break for it. But, of course, if she ran, she wouldn't get far.

It was over.

She could feel the gale wind of Whit as clearly as if she were standing in the middle of the convent's courtyard.

"Cuthbert, yeah, it's me. I haven't got her...yet. I'm working some leads. Don't worry—I'm hot on her trail," Dylan said. He waved away Serena's silent shock. "I think I can bring her in, no fuss, if you just give me a few hours. Why don't you go with the flu story—you remember, in her note?" He listened intently for a moment, nodding his head at Cuthbert's high-pitched squeal. "It'll buy you some time. Start canceling and reschedule for later. No...no, Cuthbert, don't call the cops. That would get messy. I'll bring her in myself."

He hung up.

"Where to, Princess?"

"What do you mean?"

A wicked smile stole across his face. "If you don't have a man you're meetin', you won't mind my tagging along."

IF HE HAD a weakness, it was a woman in distress. When his father died, he couldn't bear the sight of his mother straining to stay awake at the kitchen table as she ended her day at one job only to leave for her second job as soon as the dinner dishes were cleared.

He had taken a night shift in security—doing his homework in a silent factory with a German shepherd guard dog asleep at his feet.

And he had told his mother to quit her second job. She had mounted a protest but then fell silent, seeming to understand that her son had become a man. A man with a strong will and one weakness.

A weakness that had, of course, ruined him. Taken everything of value to him. His reputation. His work. His honor.

He didn't know whether he liked the princess, didn't know whether it was worth the risk to his reputation to help her, didn't know if she'd give him the slip and run off with some guy at the first opportunity, but he knew in his soul that he couldn't turn her in.

He would nudge Cuthbert, hour by hour, checking in with optimistic reports that nearly, but not quite, promised her immediate return. He would watch over her, letting her take in the harmless, simple pleasures she described. He would defend her, if necessary. He would protect her.

But he knew, in the end, he would take her back. Back to her self-imposed prison. To a man who valued freedom, it sounded like the worst sort of hell.

And it bothered him that he would be jailing her as surely as if he turned the key on her prison door.

And that, if he didn't handle this one exactly right, his weakness for a woman with a sad story would ruin him for good.

But he knew that once a man made a choice, there was no value in hesitation, in complaining or in half measures. He gave her the same wicked smile that had made other women weak in the knees. On her it seemed to have no effect.

"Where to, Princess?"

She hesitated, clearly weighing his trustworthiness against the risks. He could tell her... what?...that he was an honorable man? That he had never hurt a lady, never broken a solemn promise, never ratted on a friend, would protect her as surely as any sworn knight?

He remembered the deal he made with Cuthbert. He knew he didn't know enough to make any kind of judgment about the political machinations of the tiny European country she called home.

If she wanted freedom for one day, he was her man.

If she had planned on meeting a man, plans would have to be changed.

"How about a ball game?" she asked. "You know. American baseball."

"All right," he said. "Cubs are playing the Mets today." After a moment he asked, "By the way, is your fellow a ballplayer or something?"

He caught a glimpse of annoyance but then her expression settled into one of serene pity.

"You are so deluded. There's no man."

"Yeah, right," he muttered.

Chapter Six

"Cab."

"Bus."

"Cab."

"Bus."

"Look, Princess, you're pretty used to getting your own way, but I'm giving the orders today. We're taking a cab."

"You look to me to be the kind of man who gets his own way with women all the time. Now it's my turn. Besides, it's my memories of today that are important. I want to remember a bus."

"Cab."

"Bus."

"Cab."

"A bus is more like how people really live," she argued. "And that's what I want to have to take back with me. A memory of being an ordinary woman."

"There's nothing ordinary about you."

"I'm not sure if you meant that as a compliment."

"Take it any way you want. But you're taking a cab. Or going back to the Drake."

"Bus," she said, quickly calculating that she had just a little more room to nudge him. But not much room. "It's my day. You're just along to make sure I don't run off to meet Kevin Costner."

"You're meeting Costner?"

"Puh-leeeze! And you can take a cab whenever you want. I'll take the bus."

He shook his head—this was going to be a long day.

"Princess, somebody's going to recognize you in a crowded bus. The fewer people who see you, the better."

"Who's going to be looking for a princess on a bus?" she countered. "Besides, it's my risk. If someone recognizes me, I'll be the one with her picture on the front page of the *Star*. You can claim you were in the process of bringing me in. You'll be a hero to Cuthbert and the palace. You could probably sell your story for a lot of money."

"I'm not that mercenary."

"Aren't you? Lots of people make money that way."

"Not me. I hate the press and I do have a sense of honor," he answered, his irritation—a memory of anger—getting the better of him. She stiffened. Rubbing the hard stubble on his jaw, he wondered if what she saw was a bitter failure of a man. "All right, go on, get on the bus. Most women would be delighted to take a cab instead."

The number 36 Clark Street bus pulled up in front of them, dirt and yellowing paper swirling in its wake. The doors flipped open and the driver swung his head to stare.

"Thirty-six bus," he called out smartly.

"Get on," Dylan urged Serena.

"Here?" she asked, pointing to the steps, looking to him for reassurance. "Do I get on here? What do I do?"

"You get on the bus!"

Such a contradiction! Sometimes as imperious as, well, a princess. Sometimes as docile and needy as a child. Given the power to command with a whisper, regarded by her handlers as little more than a beautiful slave.

"Thirty-six bus," the driver said again, reaching for the lever to swing the door shut. "You gettin' on or are you just looking?"

"Come on," Dylan said. "Your carriage awaits. Don't choke now that you've got me agreeing to this."

He leapt up to the ticket box, feeling her huddle against him as he paid.

He scanned the riders. A few commuters reading their papers. Two older women with shopping bags. Three teens in the back wearing portable radio headphones. Any one of them could be a royal watcher.

But the only person who tendered Serena more than the usual urban indifference was a gray-suited businessman, who gave her the once-over as she stepped past him to take the seat Dylan had pointed to. A back-off glance from Dylan was all it took. A loud harrumph, a falsely menacing rattle of the newspaper and the princess's anonymity was guaranteed.

Dylan realized that his tracking skills had made him capable of seeing the princess. The businessman had merely seen a beautiful woman. And so would anyone else.

Serena had cropped her hair to a youthful and delicate two inches. Beautiful, yes—and he had called it right, half the women in the world would surely have similar cuts within the month. But regal? No, not at all.

No finely coifed hair. No expertly applied makeup with the signature pink champagne lipstick. No manicure with the useless half-inch talons. No heels to place her at a whisper under six feet. And no couture suits that nipped just right at her waist and showed off her million-dollar legs to advantage.

She wore a pair of faded-nearly-to-white jeans, a pair of sneakers already set with grass stains, a navy windbreaker and a white pocket T-shirt that he guessed would show up on the house charge at three for ten dollars from the hotel drugstore. A pretty woman, a head-turning woman to be sure, but to the average eye she bore only the slightest resemblance to the woman she had been just yesterday.

Even her scent, ordinarily that of the most expensive designer perfume, was now more like baby-fresh soap and talcum powder. He liked it better, he thought, breathing deeply at her shoulder as he sat down beside her.

Maybe this would work—escorting a princess under cover for the day—although he was just starting to understand that this would cost him the job.

And the money. And quite possibly everything he valued.

Because when he returned her to her cushy jail, Cuthbert would know she couldn't have pulled this one off on her own.

Money's not important, he reminded himself. He already had plenty of it. But the further erosion of his reputation disturbed him.

Why was he willing to risk that for a princess who had traded her freedom for her divorce papers?

"We've still got a few hours to kill. Where would you like to go first?" he asked, his mind trying to recall the out-of-towners kind of things she would want to do, if she knew how. "Princess?"

"I want breakfast at the coffee shop on the first floor of the Belmont Hotel," she said. "I understand they have great waffles. I've never had a waffle."

"You just had a hot dog."

"I deserve a pig-out day. I've been living on rabbit food for a long time. I've dreamed of waffles."

"How do you know about the coffee shop?"

"I read about it. We'll get off at Belmont and walk four blocks down to Lake Shore Drive," she said. "And after breakfast, we'll take the 151 bus up to Wrigley Field. We should be able to purchase tickets for today's game. I want bleachers. Cheap seats. Should cost us $8.50 each. Nothing near the skyboxes."

"You know exactly what you want," he mused, rubbing the stubble on his jaw. "I don't think I've known many women like that." He shot her a look. He hoped she didn't think he was hitting on her. She might be a princess, she might be pretty—to be honest, she looked like an angel—but sleeping with her was the last thing he needed. He was in deep enough as it was.

"Waffles. I want waffles," she said, ignoring any double reference. "I'm going to do everything I've always wanted to do today. And I know exactly how I want to do it."

Well, I'm not going to do quite everything, she conceded to herself. A hard lesson she had learned in the past eighteen years was that no one, not even a princess, got everything she wanted.

In her case, she hadn't gotten out of life the one thing she had desired above all.

Love.

To be sure, her sons loved her, and they even expressed their affection more than most teenage boys—occasionally willing to give her a big bear hug, always ready to confide their daily doubts and victories. Erik sometimes sent her whimsical notes on his official stationery when she traveled. For years, she had let Vlad win at Scrabble and these days, he let her. Both boys had returned to the palace the previous winter when she caught pneumonia— provoking the ire of the headmaster of their traditional boarding school.

And of course, the populace loved her. At least, that's what she understood from newspapers and television—and from the fan mail that kept four full-time secretaries busy. Hands reached out from crowds to her wherever she went, flowers were thrust into her arms, the shouted greetings were always kind and even the press was usually positive.

But while she adored her sons and felt a rock solid loyalty to her people, she had never experienced the one kind of love that she longed for most.

A man's love.

When she had been a bride, she had thought her husband… But no, he regarded her as a necessary, somewhat distasteful duty of his station. An heir, the spare, and then…nothing. Into her twenties, she had been approached by many suitors who were ready, nearly eager, to risk everything to have her in their beds. But she had said no, unwilling to break her vows and when her vows were dissolved, the habit of celibacy seemed too delicate to be given over to a calculating German industrialist, a Hollywood director on the make, or a bedazzled British statesman.

Even assuming she could have slipped from the watchful gaze of Bostwick and Cuthbert.

She knew she'd developed a reputation among the men of her set as being distant, a little aloof, an ice-princess. Some even considered her a tease—that last she had learned from an overheard conversation.

But she wasn't made of ice, she was warm flesh and blood.

To end this day in the arms of a man who loved her, to experience the wonders of love at its most basic and thrilling, would be a heaven she knew she could not reach.

She would have to settle for the best waffles in the world and a ball game.

As the bus rocked back and forth in traffic, Dylan's thigh grazed hers. She jerked her leg away. He apologized with a shrug. She murmured an acceptance of his apology.

It dawned on her that he could be attracted to her.

It had been a long time since a man had dared to express such a feeling, but he had proved himself in the past two weeks as a man who did what he wanted.

He wouldn't be scared off by the prospect of breaking a few rules.

She gave him a sidelong glance.

A man with strong appetites and an easy, confident way about him. If he wanted a woman, he wouldn't be afraid of rejection, wouldn't be hesitant, would be confident that she would come to him.

Another, darker possibility, came to mind.

He worked for Cuthbert.

He was an undeniably handsome and virile-looking man.

Had he been chosen by Cuthbert not so much to look for the phantom lover in her life—but to become that lover?

The embarrassment and other consequences she would suffer for an innocent day in Chicago paled beside that which she would endure for an illicit liaison with a bodyguard.

Was he sent to tempt her?

"What did Cuthbert tell you about my lover?"

He did a double take. "Your lover?"

"My supposed lover."

"You met him in India and again in Canada."

"Nothing else?"

"Your country's security and intelligence operations are rather crude. Or maybe you're just good at giving everybody the slip."

"But Cuthbert didn't say anything about whom they suspected."

"No, but I suppose I could look at any tabloid magazine for that."

She growled. "Don't you see? There's nobody. They don't even think there's anybody. Cuthbert, Bostwick, they know. They're setting you up."

"How?"

"Setting you up to…make love to me."

He gave her a dark, derisive look. "Princess, I'm

probably the only heterosexual single male in the world who's a sure bet not to want to make love to you.''

His words stung. And were meant to. She felt her cheeks crimson.

''Our stop is next,'' she said grimly. She would treat him as an aide no different from the dozens that were assigned to her at any one time.

He leaned over, raising his arm as if to encircle her. Maybe he had regretted his harsh tone, maybe he'd explain his comment. But he didn't touch her and his silence brooked no questions.

He pulled the rope to signal the driver to stop at the corner.

''I'll get out first,'' he grunted. ''You follow.''

She bridled at his rude insistence. But as she stepped from the bus, feeling the whooosh of exhaust as the bus roared away, she saw him scan the street.

''Do you see someone?'' she asked.

''No, Princess, no one's following us. I'll know when they are.''

They walked four blocks east to the Belmont Hotel. He stayed on her right, a little behind her, in the position her security aides called four o'clock. Ordinarily, she would be completely protected with three more aides at the two o'clock, ten o'clock and eight o'clock positions.

The diner was everything she expected it to be. The booths were red vinyl, distressed to look like leather. The tables were Formica edged in corrugated steel. Eight spinnable stools stood in front of the counter.

She took a seat at the window. Dylan sat across from her. The waitress, a redhead wearing a pink uniform and white running shoes, tore herself from a card she was writing.

"Seat yourself," she said and then leaned over the grill window.

"Here, Harry, you wanna sign the get well card?" she asked.

From behind the grill, Harry shrugged a noncommittal reply which the waitress took as a yes. She shoved the card and her pen into the grill window, warning him to not get any grease on the paper.

"I won't send a princess a get well card smelling like sausage," the waitress muttered as she approached Serena and Dylan. She jabbed her jeweled reading glasses up the bridge of her nose.

"Princess? What princess?" Dylan asked, steel eyes narrowing as he checked out the man reading the newspaper at the counter, the woman eating toast at the corner booth, the two teenagers drinking coffee at the back table.

"Serena. Her Royal Highness the Princess Serena," the waitress said, tossing menus on the table. "It was on the mornin' news. She's got the flu. Canceled all her appearances today. I'm sending her a get well card."

"Ask for the day off to go down to the hotel," the cook called out.

"But I'm not going!" The waitress said. "The mayor asked that the crowds at the Drake skedaddle so she can rest without a racket outside. So I'll just send her a card. She's exhausted, I say. Plum wore herself out touring the world. The jet set's like that, you know, always burning candles at both ends. Probably needs more vitamin B in her diet. Coffee?"

"Sure," Dylan said easily, his shoulders relaxing. "Susan? You want coffee."

Hiding behind the menu, Serena glanced up.

Susan?

Susan!

What a gloriously ordinary, wondrously simple name. She liked it.

"Coffee sounds good," she said, trying her best to mimic the flat, midwestern accent of the waitress, who flipped their cups over on their saucers and sloshed coffee over both.

"Know what you'll be having?"

"We'll take the waffles," Dylan said. "Two orders."

"Sausage with that?"

The waitress glanced at Serena. And gave her the once-over. Two times.

"Hey, you know, you kinda look like her."

Serena wanted to bolt, but she felt Dylan grab her

hand underneath the table. His hand was strong and his fingers squeezed. Hard.

She'd have to brazen it out.

"Like who?"

"Like Princess Serena."

"You think so?" Serena asked, feeling her voice becoming very small.

"Yeah. Hey, Harry," the waitress bellowed to the kitchen. "Don't she look like the princess?"

Chapter Seven

Serena squirmed under the waitress's frank perusal.

If it had been up to her, she would have bolted from the restaurant.

But it wasn't up to Serena.

Dylan squeezed her fingers tightly. Biting her lips, she fixed a challenging stare on the waitress.

"Yeah, I think you kinda look like her," the waitress said, chewing on her pencil.

"Really?" Dylan asked, his tone disinterested.

"Yeah, maybe if she let her hair grow out, style it a little, and put on some makeup. The princess wears the same color lipstick I do—read it in the *Star* magazine—pink champagne by Estée Lauder."

"It's actually not made by— Yow! That hurts! Stop squeezing so hard!"

"Somethin' the matter?" the waitress asked.

Serena narrowed her eyes at Dylan.

"Nothing's the matter. You were saying?"

"I was saying that you do all that, and you could be a dead ringer for her."

The cook leaned out the grill window.

"Mabel, you got that Serena on your brain," he said, shoving his white paper hat back from his brow. "This girl don't look nothing like that dolled-up foreigner. I don't mean no disrespect, young lady. You look just fine the way you are. All-American beauty. Natural-like. A man likes natural better. A man likes to know what he's getting in a woman."

"I'm telling you, Harry, she could be the Princess Serena's twin sister."

"Mabel, are you putting in an order or am I goin' on break?"

"Harry, you don't have to use that tone of voice with me!"

Mabel snapped up the menus. As soon as she was out of earshot, Dylan released Serena's fingers.

"Close call," he whispered.

She rubbed her hands together and glanced down at her lap. He had branded her wrists pink with his touch.

She wondered if she should remind him that a commoner never, ever touched a royal without express permission, rarely granted. She decided not to. He had forced her to hold her ground. And he had won her second breakfast for her.

"Don't surrender before you have to," he added. "And don't run while you still can hold your ground. You did all right."

"What would we have done if she had recognized me?"

"Brazen it out. Deny, deny, deny. 'I'm not a princess, but thank you for the compliment,' is what you say. You want your day bad enough, don't you?"

"I do. Today is wonderful."

It was wonderful, she decided, as Mabel laid their piled-high plates on the table minutes later. A crisp waffle with a scoop of butter melting into the squares. Smothering it with fragrant maple syrup, Serena bit in.

"These waffles are great," she moaned. "Worth everything."

"You can make them yourself," he said, ignoring his plate. "Plenty of people do. All it takes is a waffle iron."

"I'll have Lord Cuthbert order one immediately. I wonder if I can learn to cook. I'll have plenty of time for new hobbies."

"Here," Dylan said, reaching across the table. He touched his napkin to her lips. "You've got syrup on you."

The offhanded gesture meant nothing to him, she was sure, but it embarrassed and unnerved her. She looked away. Right into the waitress's inquisitive eyes. Mabel looked like the kind of woman who wasn't above eavesdropping.

Don't surrender before you have to.

And don't run while you still can fight.

"I'M STUFFED," she announced as they hit the street an hour later. "I never want to even look at food again."

"That's what everybody says when they eat that much," Dylan said. "But it was a brilliant strategy."

"Strategy? What strategy?"

"I overheard our waitress telling the cook that the Princess Serena only eats fruits and vegetables to maintain her size-two figure. If she had any doubts about you, that second order of waffles made up her mind that you are a commoner."

"For today, I am a commoner. And a very happy one."

They boarded the 151 bus and headed north toward the Cubs playing field. By unspoken pact, they didn't talk about Serena—rather, Dylan kept up a running patter of Chicago stories.

There was the apartment building where his best friend from high school lived. There was the church his family attended. On that block—Serena quickly turned her head so she wouldn't miss it—was the nursery school, torn down years ago to make room for a Laundromat.

Over there, on that corner he got into his first fight, defending a girl who had been teased mercilessly by a pack of boys. Serena leaned over to catch a glimpse of the corner and got caught up in his scent—a masculine melding of musk and citrus.

"Did you win?" she asked with a nonchalance that hid how he unsettled her by his nearness.

He laughed easily. "I won back her book bag, broke the nose of the ringleader and she ran away, still sobbing."

"Not much of a thanks for a knight in shining armor."

"Oh, I got my thanks. Seven years later, I ran into her in a bar my buddies from work took me to. She put her arms around me and told me that she was going to take all night to express her gratitude."

"And did she?"

He opened his mouth to answer and then closed it again. He had obviously forgotten himself, nearly blurting out the entire story.

And it must be quite a story.

She felt an impish delight at his embarrassment.

"I...I shouldn't say," he answered, running his fingers through his errant hair. "I was young and foolish and..."

"You're not anymore."

"I'm not young but I guess I'm still foolish."

"Have you ever been married?"

"No, I'm not that foolish."

"No serious girlfriend?"

"Nope."

"Never?" Serena asked, intrigued by the notion that what he wasn't saying about himself was more important than what he was willing to talk about.

"A couple I thought might turn into something

special. I used to think one day a woman would come into my life and I'll be sure of myself...and I'd be right. But it's never happened that way. I don't think it ever will—and I can live with that. I figure my sister Charlotte will have kids and that'll have to do as family for me.'' He regarded her thoughtfully. ''Why are you asking all this?''

''I was wondering how regular people do this sort of thing, you know, fall in love, get married.''

''They don't plan any of it. It just happens.''

''But how can you ensure that you don't fall in love with someone who is wrong for you?''

A dark look settled on his face, an unexpected flash of bitterness and then a tight set to his jaw.

''You don't know. You don't know until it's too late to do anything about it.''

''Oh, dear, that sounds terrible.''

''Sometimes it is,'' he agreed. ''Now fair's fair. How did you...?''

''It was arranged,'' she said matter-of-factly. ''Oh, I know the press made a huge deal about this fairy-tale romance. But it wasn't like that. My parents informed me I was marrying the prince. And I was happy to do it.''

She recalled the appointment with the palace physician. An odd mixture of the modern and barbaric, the visit included a humiliating examination to confirm her virginity and ability to bear children as well as a high-tech DNA test to detect any genetic weaknesses. She had come through it all with flying colors and her naive romanticism irreparably in tatters.

"I was seventeen," she continued, glancing away as the woman sitting across the aisle hoisted her shopping bags up and waddled to the front of the bus. "I was so young I wasn't wise enough to see how it would all turn out. And, as the big day approached, I got caught up in the romance of a royal wedding."

"So did the rest of the world."

"But it sounds so much more romantic to do things the American way. You meet someone, get to know them, fall in love, and then..."

"No, it's not any more romantic than what you went through," he corrected brusquely. "And there's only two kinds of Americans—the cold-blooded ones and the ones who kid themselves into thinking they're not cold-blooded. The romantic fools."

"That sounds very cynical."

"A cynic is just someone who doesn't flinch at the truth."

"And which category do you belong in?"

"I kidded myself. Once. And it's never happened again. And it won't. So I suppose I'm the cold-blooded type."

She studied his face, and if she had wanted to, if she had felt comfortable enough, she could have touched the sadness at the corners of his eyes.

But something stopped her, something in his face said, back off.

She looked straight ahead, to the back of the straw hat of the woman seated a couple seats in front of them.

"Once, huh?"

He bit off a grunt that sounded like "yeah."

"We're two of a kind," she observed. "Once was enough for me, too."

She looked up at him then, his eyes worn by wry understanding, featherlight lines marring his tan. She wanted to confide in him, to meet him with the truth, all of it. But then she remembered.

He was Cuthbert's hire.

And he said—only once.

"Is your job to fool me into fooling myself?" She asked.

"How so?"

"To fool myself that I want to make love to you."

He shook his head. "I keep telling you, Princess, I'm the last man on earth for that stuff. I wouldn't make love to you if you begged me to."

"You don't have to say it in quite those terms."

"All right. You've got a great pair of legs, a very nice smile—with or without the pink champagne—and you're just the shade of blonde I go for. But I'm not making love to you. Under any circumstances."

"I'm not asking you to. And I never beg."

WHEN THEY GOT off the bus, Dylan pulled the cell phone from his pocket and made another call to Cuthbert.

"It's a madhouse here," Cuthbert lamented. "A pharmaceutical company just sent a crate of aspirin for Her Royal Highness. The orange growers association delivered ten cases of juice. The crowds are blocking traffic, chanting her name until I think I might go mad. I can't even begin to describe what all these flowers are doing to my sinuses. Where is she, MacPhail?"

"North side," Dylan said vaguely, looking up to meet Serena's amused expression. She was starting to enjoy herself. "North side of the city, Cuthbert. Just give me a few more hours. Better to be sneezing like crazy than to have the police and the press working the story of her disappearance."

"I suppose you're right," Cuthbert said gloomily, and then there was a muffled roar. "Oh, dear, someone get those delphiniums out of here. They're simply oozing allergens. Has she met anyone?"

"No."

"She's all on her own?"

"Yes."

"Ghastly. Simply ghastly."

"You sound like you'd be happier if she was meeting a lover."

There was a long pause. Dylan regretted the dig and wondered if he had gone too far in goading the lord.

"Why would I ever want the mother of the two heirs to the throne to besmirch her royal station?" Cuthbert asked coolly.

"I'm just thinking about what the tabloids tell me, about Franco's troubles getting people to like Lady Jane," Dylan said, recovering quickly. "You want me to be well-informed, don't you?"

"I suppose so. But, MacPhail, we're paying you a helluva lot of money—we need you to do more than just read the tabloids. Get that princess back here! And if you can't get her, get pictures. Explicit pictures. With both of them. Compromised."

"Pictures? Don't you think pictures are a little...sick?"

"No, my dear MacPhail, pictures would be heavenly. It would make up for all this... Achooo!"

"I'll bring her back," Dylan promised, suppressing his repugnance at Cuthbert's suggestion. "No pictures, though."

"Too bad."

"Get well soon."

"I'll only feel better when she's where she belongs. And when you bring her back in, I swear I'll put her in cuffs if that's what I have to do to keep her in line!"

Dylan bit back a retort. He kept his voice genial and upbeat.

"Don't worry, Cuthbert, I'm following up some solid leads. I'll have her in by this evening."

"Are you going to string him along like that for

the whole day?'' Serena asked as he flipped the phone shut. She stepped onto the curb to allow a mother with a double stroller to pass by.

''If I told him I didn't expect to have you back until tomorrow, he'd send someone else looking,'' Dylan explained, tugging her back onto the sidewalk just as a taxi passed. ''This way, he is never quite convinced that he needs to do anything but wait.''

''But you won't turn me in? Not before I'm ready?''

''I promise. But if you try to give me the slip...''

''There is no lover.''

''Then there should be no problem. I promise the whole twenty-four hours.''

''In the early days of my country, the knights would make a blood oath of loyalty.''

Against a drumbeat in his head that told him No!, he took her hand, guiding her fingers to his chest.

He traced a cross on his shirt, teasing his senses with the pressure of her touch.

''Cross my heart and hope to die,'' he said, recovering his male confidence. His voice would sound as smooth as the finest whiskey, but he felt a catch. He grazed the smooth, ivory skin of the back of her hand. ''Stick a needle in my eye.'' He brought her hand up to his face, opening her fingers and pressing his lips to the cool flesh of her palm. ''If I ever tell a lie.''

She gasped.

''That's the closest us Americans come to spilling

their blood for a promise to a princess,'' he said, drawing her fingers into a fist and relinquishing her.

Studying her face, he knew he had startled her by turning her hand, by kissing her palm. Hell, he had startled himself. Such a personal gesture, when she expected the more formal kiss on the back of the hand and he had expected nothing more from himself than a few gruff words.

So the princess wasn't as experienced with men as she thought she was.

And he had lost his touch with women. It had been a long time. He promised himself that when this day was over he would find himself a nice, sweet girl for the night. Blonde, curvy, with no expectations stretching beyond breakfast the next morning.

But for today, he had a princess on his hands.

All the rumors and innuendo about her having lovers—he wondered. Could the rumors be untrue? Her inexperience patently obvious as she rubbed the flesh of her palm, thinking he didn't notice. How could he have taken advantage of this innocent? How could he have lost it like that?

He wondered at the girl she must have been, her wedding portrait now bubbling into memory. Eighteen years before, the picture had been plastered all over the papers. She wore a dress that fluttered with lace and high hopes. Tender pink rosebuds had been threaded into her hair—and the style had sparked a fashion rage for months after the royal nuptials. But it was her smile that he remembered now most clearly.

A smile edged not with shyness, as most people thought, but with terror. He knew that now.

He wondered at the man, at the country, at the traditions of marriage, that had crushed that hope and made her into his kind.

His kind of cold-blooded cynic.

"Excuse me," someone said at his shoulder. Dylan realized he and Serena had drifted to block the entrance to a record store.

He took her elbow and guided her out of the sidewalk traffic.

"Cheap seats, huh?" he asked. "Left field or right field?"

"Left field," she said. "I want to catch a home run."

They walked up the block to the ticket counter at Wrigley Field. He heard a frantic yelling of his name. He turned around to see a friend from the old neighborhood running toward them.

"Remember what I said, Princess, about knowing when someone's following us?"

"Yes."

"Well, just keep in mind—you're Susan. You'd better learn to call me Dylan. And, by the way, we're on a date. We like each other. A lot."

"That's going to require acting skills I simply do not possess."

"Aarggghh!"

"Hey, buddy!" A squat, dark-haired man bellowed from across the street. "Dylan, it's me! Rocco!"

The man trotted toward them, bringing traffic to a halt, exchanging a good-natured oath with a cabbie who squealed to a halt bare inches from him.

"Rocco, good to see you," Dylan said, slapping his hand against his friend's. "You here for the game?"

"Yeah, that's why I became a schoolteacher," Rocco said, looking speculatively at Serena. "Only job I know where a man gets his summers off to watch the Cubbies. What are you doin' here, MacPhail? You're the only man I've ever known who'd rather work than take in the Cubs."

"No, I'm taking the afternoon off to see the game," Dylan said, and he instinctively reached out to Serena.

Rocco caught the gesture and gave Serena the once-over.

He whistled softly.

"Oh, Dylan, your momma is going to be mighty pleased."

Chapter Eight

"Well, uh, actually, Rocco, my mom doesn't know I'm in town."

Rocco discounted that possibility with a brisk wave of his pudgy hand. "Oh, I'll betcha she knows. You were written up in one of those magazines they sell at the 7-Eleven," he said. "Wait a minute, if Princess Serena is holed up at the Drake Hotel sick as a dog, how come you're here?"

"When she got sick, I got the afternoon off," Dylan said, casually pulling Serena into his embrace. "My boss isn't going anywhere and I wanted to show Susan what the natives here like to do."

"I'm...um... Her Highness's secretary," Serena improvised.

Rocco cocked his head. "I was wondering about the resemblance. Anybody ever tell you that you and the princess favor each other?"

"All the people from my country look alike," Susan assured him.

Dylan kissed her forehead. "And just think, Rocco, she's going out with me!"

"Yeah, who woulda thought you could attract a real nice girl?"

She shot Dylan a glance to inform him that he didn't have to playact this affectionate dating stuff quite so effectively. But he had already turned around to buy tickets.

"Two," Dylan said to the person behind the ticket window. "Make 'em bleachers. Left field."

"Great, you'll be with us!" Rocco exclaimed. "The whole gang's here. The original bleacher bums. Tony, Stephen, Eddie—you should know, Susan, that Dylan is our golden boy. Most successful product of our 'hood. I'm not saying I'm a schlub. I teach math at Clemente High. But Dylan, well, he's in a class by himself."

"I've always thought that about him," Serena said dryly.

Rocco nodded vigorously.

"Here he is, picked for the Secret Service right out of college. Covering the president, then going on to work on his own—rock stars, ambassadors, billionaires. Can you imagine that? And he's always had enough time for the gang. Hey, Dylan, what's the princess really like?"

"She's a real...witch," he said, a mischievous smile playing across his face. "Wouldn't you say so, Susan?"

She bit back a retort and gave Rocco her trademark dazzling smile. "Oh, yes. Totally demanding. Throws temper tantrums when her shoes aren't arranged in alphabetical order."

"And she seems so sweet and innocent." Rocco shook his head. "What you're describing ain't nothing like what she seems in public."

"Night and day," Dylan muttered.

"How long you worked for her, Susan?"

"Forever, it seems. Way too long."

AFTER INTRODUCING his girlfriend Susan to Tony, Stephen and Eddie and a dozen other bleacher bums he knew from the old neighborhood, Dylan quickly outlined the rules of baseball. The other men chimed in at every opportunity with the exceptions, the strategies, the records, the history of the game, and the personalities of the players.

"Don't worry, Susan, I know the game sounds confusing to a non-American," Rocco cautioned. "But by the end of the first inning, you'll catch on."

As the bleacher bums tried to explain the designated hitter rule, a good-natured argument erupted. Tony thought it was an unfair advantage to teams with a better pitcher pool. Stephen and Eddie thought it made no difference. Rocco thought it would be the end of baseball.

"Yeah, but you also thought night games at Wrigley Field would be the end of baseball," Tony accused.

Dylan's date garnered a double take when she set

the designated hitter matter to rest with a well-reasoned explanation of the differing game statistics for teams affected by the rule and the impact the dispute over the rule had had on the All Stars game.

"Whoa, you didn't tell us she was an expert!" Tony exclaimed, making a courtly bow to Serena that was earned and not protocol.

"Marry her immediately," Stephen counseled, with a wink and a smile for Serena. "If you don't, I will. I mean, where else will a man ever find such a combination of beauty, brains and an understanding of the game?"

Serena joined in the men's laughter. Dylan threw up his scorecard in an exaggerated gesture of defeat. Tony's attention was distracted by the wild call of the soda pop vendor.

"It's your turn to buy," he told Rocco.

"No way," Rocco protested. "It's Eddie's turn."

"Not me. I picked up the tab when we lost to Philadelphia."

Dylan pulled a twenty from his wallet. "Here, guys, I haven't been to a game in a while," he said. "I'm probably behind on picking up my share."

"Darn right you're behind," Rocco said, snapping up the bill. "Whatcha drinking?"

With Rocco and Eddie occupied with the soda pop vendor and Tony searching the stands for the hot dog man, Dylan figured he was safe from eavesdroppers.

"Where'd you learn all about baseball?" he asked.

"My secret lover is a professional ballplayer."

Dylan did a double take.

"Gotcha," Serena said, poking him in the ribs. "It was actually Bostwick."

"Lady Bostwick? I would never figure her for a baseball fan."

"No, no, no. I told her I wanted to be able to talk intelligently about baseball with the mayor. She put together a report and even supplied me with a couple of videos of past games."

"Amazing."

"I've researched every facet of today," Serena added proudly. "I've learned everything I can about Chicago. Memorized street maps, bus routes, store locations, restaurants. I wanted to be totally free."

"Freedom isn't just a city or a day. It's a feeling, how you feel about yourself. It's a feeling worth dying for."

"What an Americanism," Serena sniffed.

"You think there's something more important?"

"For me, it's the love I have for my sons and my country. I would do anything for them—including giving up my freedom. And I don't think I'm different from any other mother. Or any other patriot."

"Come on, lovebirds, stop your yapping and get on your feet," Rocco leaned over to interrupt. He handed Serena and Dylan two gigantic plastic cups of soda. "They got the players on the field. Time for the national anthem."

She stood up with the men and listened to the stirring tribute to the American flag. The bleacher bums made up in enthusiasm what they lacked in musical talent. Rocco said the national anthem always made him cry.

"Play ball!" Tony shouted as the crowd erupted into cheers for the Cubs as they took their positions on the field.

A soft touch for the vendors who roamed the aisles, Dylan bought Serena a box of popcorn, a souvenir cap, a pennant and a stuffed Cubbie bear. She hugged the bear to her chest and her ear-to-ear grin made him want to be the one to put a smile on her face every day.

Whoa, Dylan! he thought. Pull back and think.

This isn't a woman named Susan. This isn't a working-class girl within your reach. This is a princess. A real princess who has an ironclad appointment with a solitary future, where there wouldn't be many smiles like the one on her face right now.

And before you go feeling sorry for her, he thought, *remember that she chose that future.*

He shifted uncomfortably, jerked at the collar of his T-shirt and tried to concentrate on the batter.

"What do you think of baseball?" Eddie asked Serena as the inning ended with no runs.

"It's great!" Serena said.

"In high school, we came out to Wrigley field

every chance we got,'' Eddie explained. "We'd ditch school, I used to pay my girlfriend to do my homework for me. We never missed a spring opener. 'Course, after Dylan's dad passed on, he didn't get to join us as much as he would have liked.''

"And then he got in the Secret Service right after school,'' Tony added, shoving his hand into Eddie's popcorn box. "We missed him even more but we welcomed him back when they let him go.''

"Damn shame about that,'' Rocco shook his head. "Pardon my French, but he was...he wasn't treated fairly.''

"What do you mean wasn't treated fairly?'' Serena asked. "Dylan, what are they talking about?''

"Uh-oh,'' Stephen said. "Now you guys have done it.''

"Sorry, man,'' Rocco said.

Dylan stared broodingly out onto the field.

"Rocco, Tony, she don't know nothing about it,'' Eddie said. "And it's not our place to tell her.''

"Tell me what?'' Serena asked.

"Sorry, man,'' Rocco repeated.

"Yeah, sorry,'' Tony said. "I thought everybody knew about it.''

"No need to be sorry. It's not that big of a deal. What's done is done,'' Dylan said evenly. "Susan, I was forced out of the Secret Service.''

"It was a setup!'' Rocco growled.

"Still, it meant a fifteen-year career down the drain. Happened last year.''

Serena felt sick to her stomach, and it wasn't the hot dog, the double order of waffles, or even the popcorn, the box for which she felt slip from her fingers to the ground. She wasn't sure if she felt sympathy or wariness or a flat sense of foreboding.

"Forced out?"

"He coulda stayed," Tony said. "He coulda fought it."

"Tony, shut up," Eddie warned. "Let Dylan be the one to explain it."

Serena studied Dylan's profile. Who was this American? Could he harm her? Had she done or said anything that would endanger her boys? Had she trusted him when others had found him untrustworthy?

The other men avoided her eyes, studying the game with an intensity that even the most ardent fan ordinarily wouldn't possess.

"Don't worry. I'm not going to betray you," Dylan said softly, refusing to meet her eyes. "I wasn't a good Secret Service agent. I made a mistake, but I was serious when I told you I'd protect you. My oath means something. It means everything to me."

She smiled—a bit wobbly but still brave. In the back of her mind, she wondered... And even as she got caught up in the excitement of the game and the men forgot they had said anything disturbing about their friend, she felt a niggling worry.

She'd have to ask for a full explanation afterward of course. It could be drugs or a drinking problem, or maybe he just didn't follow orders, or he couldn't hack the discipline. But she'd have to know.

AFTER NINE GRUELING innings, the Cubs stood poised for defeat. Two outs, three men on base, down four runs, a rookie at bat.

The bleacher bums kept their bravado up. Part of the charm of being a Cubs fan was weathering—no, welcoming—the losses. After two strikes, Rocco asked if anybody else wanted to go to the Cubbie Lounge across the street for a beer.

"Guy's gonna hit a homer next," Dylan said, suddenly shaking the quiet gloom which had settled over him.

"Yeah, right, Dylan," Tony muttered amiably. "You could always predict 'em. But this time you're dead wrong. Guy's a rookie, never even gotten on base this season."

"Stand up," Dylan whispered to Serena.

She glanced at him, nearly asking him why, and then obeyed.

"Stand on the seat in front of me."

"Sit down," Rocco brayed. "There ain't gonna be no homer. Even if there was, it would only put off the inevitable. We're toast. We're finished. We're the Cubs. We thrive on defeat. We haven't won a pennant in more than three decades."

She stepped onto the seat and he stood behind her, slipping his hands underneath her arms. Guiding her fingers to open. She felt the texture of his flesh. She wondered if he felt the electricity between them—then decided it was her imagination, her neediness, her own excitement.

"Close your eyes and tell the batter to give you the ball," Dylan said softly.

"Jeez, would you two si' down?" Tony demanded.

"Do it, Serena. Do it now."

She closed her eyes. She pulled her concentration from the feel of Dylan pressing against her back.

Bring it here, batter, batter.

Bring it here.

Crack!

"This could be it," Rocco said, scrambling to his feet and showering his popcorn on Dylan and Serena. "This could be it!"

"Nah, it couldn't be," Eddie cautioned.

Tony repeated a childhood prayer, his words growing louder and louder until as the ball headed toward the bleachers, he shrieked his pleas to the heavens.

Twenty thousand fans were on their feet.

"Open your eyes, Serena."

Her eyes flew open just as the ball slapped into her hand, shocked and tingling. He cupped his hand over hers, rubbing the pain away against the skin of the ball.

The crowd went wild. Rocco and Tony shot up into the air and butted their chests together. Popcorn rained down from a fan's overturned box. The floorboards beneath her feet vibrated.

"You said you wanted to experience everything! How about catching a home run?" Dylan shouted.

She opened her hand to the dirty, grass-stained ball with burgundy stitching. It seemed imbued with more regalness than that found on the finest royal robe.

And then she did a most unroyal thing. A most impulsive act. She flung her free arm around Dylan. She had never felt more wonderful being…being his for the day.

His strong arms wound around her waist, lifting her high in the air. The ecstatic fans became a blur, their cheers like the purr of a limousine's idling engine, and as she slid down, down until her toes touched the cement, he did not relinquish her. She looked up at his face, his expression unexpectedly tender and yet passionate. Her new baseball cap toppled off her head.

And then he kissed her.

His mouth stilled her trembling hesitation, and then just as she calmed, he drew away.

A fire ignited within her, its flames swirling up from her belly, until her lips felt scorched. She wanted more, more than the kiss of a fan's pandemonium.

Just this once to be kissed within an inch of her life.

He knew. He must know, as his eyes caught hers.

He didn't draw back, didn't flinch, but pulled her sharply to him as if the passion of the moment were of his design. He kissed the softest part of her lip and then the ragged edge where she so often bit her own flesh in nervousness.

She thought she might cry out from the shocking need, and he responded, plunging his tongue between her lips, searching and finding each secret sense.

A hot, wet, long, slow kiss that took her body soaring.

Rocco tugged at her sleeve.

"Come on, you two, we've still got the tenth inning to play!" he groused. "Ask Dylan when the next homer's gonna come."

Brought to sudden self-consciousness, utterly unused to a lack of decorum in public, Serena jerked away from Dylan's embrace.

And then she saw it.

Or rather, him.

The photographer.

On the lowest bleacher, turning away indifferently as soon as he had captured their kiss on film.

A plaintive wail erupted in her throat. She was such a fool, she thought angrily. Such a selfish fool. She had given up everything, her country's well-being, even her sons' future, for a kiss.

DYLAN LUNGED OVER the rows of bleacher seats two at a time, jumping onto the stairwell just as the photographer hit the bottom step.

"Hey! You there!"

The photographer startled. He was short, wore a T-shirt expressing his brand preference in beer and had a Nikon camera that Dylan guessed was worth over a thousand dollars. The man was a professional.

It was worse than he thought, but Dylan still hoped he had enough money on him—he figured it would take a lot.

"You talkin' to me?" the photographer challenged, jutting his chin out like a wise guy.

"Yeah, I'm talking to you. I'll buy the film out of that camera."

"Aren't you the guy I just snapped? Your girl just caught the homer?"

"Yeah."

"Well, might as well give me your name," the man said, reaching into his pocket for a small notepad. "Hers, too. I can guarantee you're both going to be on the front page of the sports section of the *Tribune* tomorrow."

"A hundred bucks for the film," Dylan said, pulling his money clip out. He slipped a crisp bill off the top, catching the photographer's disdainful expression. "All right, two hundred."

"No way."

"Three?"

The photographer drew closer, staring hungrily at the hundred-dollar bills.

Whistling sharply, he shook his head. "You gotta be kiddin' me. Don't you want your shot at fifteen minutes of fame?"

"I already had mine. Long time ago. I don't want any more."

"What's the picture to you?"

Dylan thought fast.

"You're a man of the world," he said, slipping two more bills out. "My girlfriend and I... Well, you know how it can be."

"Now I gotcha," the photographer said, snatching the bills. "Don't want your old lady to know, huh?"

"Husband, actually," Dylan said dryly. "Ex-husband."

"Whatever," the photographer said, winding the film back and opening his camera. "Don't think I make this deal for everyone. I had a lot of great shots."

He dropped the film into Dylan's outstretched hand. Dylan shoved the film into his jeans pocket.

"You might consider not taking your girlfriend in public if you don't want to be seen," the photographer called after him. "Get a hotel room for that kind of stuff."

As he walked back to Serena, Dylan brought his emotions into check. No more kisses. He couldn't let it happen again. She had too much at stake. And he did, too.

I'd better take this as a warning, he thought. A stop sign. A yellow crime scene ribbon.

'Cause I've been down this very same path before. Losing everything for a woman.

He found her pacing the aisle when he returned. Rocco and the gang looked up from the action, curious and congratulatory, but quickly distracted by the unfolding drama of the tenth inning.

"You're safe, Princess," Dylan said softly.

Her relief was palpable, tears springing to her eyes as she repeated her thanks so many times he started to wonder at how much she regretted their kiss.

She had a lot at stake and he knew the feeling—he had as much to lose.

He wouldn't blame her if she considered him at fault. And he had to remind himself that she wasn't the one to blame.

"Sorry I put you in that position," he said, dropping the roll of film into her outstretched hand. "I should have told you to duck."

She put the film in her pocket, and her face grew still and calm. If he was expecting a thank you, he was disappointed—her next words were a chilly command.

"It's time for you to escort me back to the hotel."

Chapter Nine

It shouldn't matter to him. It was her business what she chose to do. He shouldn't care one way or another. But he did. And her words cut into him with as much force and surprise as the bullet he had taken for the U.N. ambassador scant months before.

"Back to the hotel? What do you mean, go back? The day's just beginning. What about dinner? What about dancing? What about…?"

"It's over," she snapped. "You may escort me back to the Drake immediately."

No way, he thought. No way she really wanted to go.

He reflexively employed every weapon at his disposal. A native, wicked charm. A boyish grin. His baby blues. The pressure of emotion.

"Serena, please reconsider. Don't you want to see the end of the game? Come on, the Cubbies might still win."

She shook her head implacably.

"It doesn't matter how the game turns out," Serena said crisply. "We're going. At least I am."

"How 'bout a beer first at the Cubbie Lounge? You might even get to see some of the players stop in," he said, blocking her path. He didn't like to use his size to intimidate, but he had no choice. His smile hadn't changed her mind. She wouldn't look him in the eyes. And her emotions seemed focused in one direction—out of here. "The Cubbie Lounge. A Chicago tradition. It's on one of your maps. Corner of—"

"Clark and Armitage," she finished his sentence. "We're still going. Besides, don't you think it's a little early for a beer?"

"Yeah, so you can have a soda."

"We're going."

He jumped to block her way. "Don't you think it's going to look kind of funny for you to leave now? Don't you think my friends will put two and two together?"

"And what? Come up with four?"

"They'll figure out who you are."

"I don't think they care who I am," Serena said. She glanced over at the men, their eyes trained on the players like hungry puppies following a tantalizing bit of meat.

"It doesn't look like my departure is going to result in any spurts of deductive reasoning," Serena said.

"Okay, look, you're worried about the photographer. But it's no big deal," he pleaded. "I gave you the film. No one's gonna know about this."

"To the hotel," she said, staring pointedly at his hand gripping her shoulder.

He followed her gaze. His hand looked clumsy, too large, out of place, somehow completely wrong.

Everything that usually worked on women, worked so easily that he sometimes felt he was cheating at life, hadn't done anything to dissuade her. Not the smile, not the eyes, not the darn near begging. She had withdrawn her permission for him to act as her equal.

He lifted his hand, tightened it into a fist and let it drop uselessly to his side. "All right, Princess," he conceded. "Have it your way. Let's go back. I didn't want to stay to see the Cubs win anyhow."

"Liar."

"All right, maybe I did. Maybe I did a whole lot. But you've taken that away from me now."

"I extend my heartfelt sympathy to you in this hour of tragedy."

"Yeah, right."

He was a proud man, he wasn't used to begging. So he didn't do a very good job of it.

"Please, Princess, please stay. I don't know why I care one way or another, but we were having some fun. No need to shut it down."

She shook her head.

With a sudden sweep of irritation, he knew he just

wasn't going to humiliate himself by trying again. He made terse goodbyes to his friends.

"How can you leave!?" Tony shrieked. "We're dangling here in the tenth inning with a shot at a win!"

"Aw, let him alone," Rocco advised without taking his eyes off the field. "He's got a beautiful woman and probably only a few hours until the princess is back on her feet. Go on out of here, Dylan. Pleased to meet you, Susan. Come on back to the old neighborhood again and I'll have my wife make us all some dinner one night...." he added, and then stood to watch a line drive that threatened to become a double for the Mets.

Serena waited until she was sure that Dylan was a step behind her and then she took the railing of the stairs.

"Hey, don't you want that stuff?" Dylan asked, gesturing to their abandoned seats. The cap he had bought her, the stuffed Cubbie bear, the red-white-and-blue pennant.

"No, I don't think it's a very good idea for me to keep souvenirs," she said. She struggled to keep her face impassive as she dropped the home run ball into his hand. "I really don't want to explain any more than I have to."

"Maybe you'll want this later," he said, slipping it into the pocket of his jacket.

"I think not," she lied in a clipped, cultured voice.

Against the roar of an excited crowd, she slipped down the steps and into the corridor leading to the street, a step ahead of Dylan. A good thing, because she didn't want him to see her naked anguish.

"I don't get you, Serena. One minute, you're telling me you need your freedom, the next you're giving me the pampered princess treatment."

"I don't have to explain myself to anyone," she said, quickening her step down the long, dark corridor to the exit. "Least of all you."

He grabbed her elbow, jerking her into his embrace.

"What was it that's got you so spooked? You stared down that waitress."

"So?" She grimaced. She shook her head from side to side to avoid his eyes. He pulled her closer, and she was forced to acknowledge his gaze.

"Your freedom meant something to you this morning. You were willing to be scared and to tough it out. Now you're jumping right back behind your prison walls. You walk back into that hotel now and they'll know you're under their thumbs for the rest of your life."

"And they'll be right," she said, splaying her fingers against his chest, struggling vainly against his firm grip.

"But I got you the film," he repeated. "You don't need to run away."

"And what if the palace finds out?"

"How are they going to find out? There's no pictures."

"Somebody'll recognize me."

"Didn't you listen to me this morning? Deny, deny, deny. That was some other northern European princess in the left field bleachers."

"No, they'll know."

"Who cares if they did? You went to a ball game. That hardly counts as treason, even in a country as backward as yours. Sure, it won't look good if word got out that you're playing hooky when everyone thinks you're bedridden. But that'll be smoothed over in a month—that's what public relations people are for. I put myself out on the line for you, Princess, and I want to know, just for myself, what the hell got you so spooked."

She shook her head, closing her eyes so that she would not meet his. Because he might see the truth...the whole truth.

"I am a princess and I must return to my official duties. I have been quite remiss."

The words—chilly, remote, yet hinting a fiery resolve—brought him to his senses. He relinquished her.

Did he think she was spoiled? Cruel? A schemer?

Could she afford to care what he thought?

She put her hand on the cold metal bar of the exit door.

"Princess," he said softly, his voice a golden caress in a dark, dark night of her spirit. "Princess, that kiss scared you, didn't it?"

She didn't answer.

"You've never had a man kiss you like that, have you?"

She shoved open the bar. The metal scraped and wheezed. The raw sunlight was like a slap in the face. The air smelled of hot dogs and car exhaust.

"Don't you read the papers?" she said, tilting her chin upward. "I've been linked with half a dozen men within the last year alone."

And she didn't dare glance back at the man who could, with just another kiss, bring down a kingdom.

"I'VE GOT HER."

"Her Royal Highness? Bravo, MacPhail."

"I'll bring her in."

"Where was she?"

"North side. I'll let her explain."

"Was she...with someone?"

"No, she was on her own. I said I'll let her do the explaining."

"No lover, huh?"

"You called it wrong, Cuthbert. All wrong. There was no man."

"Still, it's marvelous that you've got her. Quite tip-top. Sorry I ever doubted you. You're well worth every penny we're paying you."

"Thanks for the compliment," Dylan said sourly.

"I hope you'll still feel that way when I bill you. I'll bring her in now."

"Dandy!" Cuthbert's voice dropped to just above a whisper. "Did she give you any fight?"

"No. She's a princess, through and through. Just wanted a day to see how the common folk live."

"Ugh. Why would anyone ever want to do that?"

"Yeah, I guess that's the conclusion she reached. Look, we'll be there in twenty minutes."

There was a long silence.

"MacPhail, I just thought of something wretched but I'm sure that with your quick wits you'll know what to do."

"What is it?"

"How do you plan to get through the crowds around the hotel without causing Her Royal Highness and the palace any…undue embarrassment? After all, she's supposed to be up here nursing a flu."

"Cuthbert, that's your call. Front lobby, kitchen door, fire escape. You tell me where you want her deposited…."

Dylan glanced at the princess, sitting sullen and worn on the bench next to the bus stop.

"Well, MacPhail, old buddy, uh, give me some time to, uh, work out the logistics. We're going to have to clear a route," Cuthbert replied. "What's your location? Give me your phone number."

"We're on the north side. And my cell phone number is…" He suddenly felt unaccountably reluctant to give Cuthbert the number, perhaps because he had never shared the number with anyone except his mother—and she only called in the direst emergencies. "Cuthbert, I'll check in with you later. Think you can have a secure route put together in one hour?"

"Righto," Cuthbert agreed, his relief palpable. "But, do me a favor, MacPhail. Keep her out of public. I wouldn't want any slipups. And hang on to her!"

Dylan shoved the slim phone into his pocket and slumped onto the bench next to Serena.

She looked as forbidding as if she were sitting for her portrait and as fragile as if she were a little girl awaiting her punishment for having run away.

"Did you work things out with Cuthbert?"

"Yeah, they've got some logistics problems to iron out about how to slip you into the Drake without attracting attention," Dylan explained. "We'll hook up with Cuthbert in an hour and I'll take you in."

"And until then?"

"We're going home. My mom's, actually. I need some downtime. You probably do, too."

"I don't think that's a very wise idea."

"'Fraid I'm going to touch you again? Well, I'm not. I lost my head for a moment, but it won't happen again. I'm not your type and you're not mine. I'm blue jeans and you're evening gowns. I'm hot dogs and cold beer and you're...whatever they have at a palace."

"You're a he-man who would lay down his life for his freedom and I'm a scared little rabbit."

"You said it, I didn't."

"But you're thinking that."

"No, actually, I was thinking you're beautiful and charming, a great catcher and an even better kisser, but you don't have more than a day to get to know me. And I don't want to get to know any woman right now."

"Not even for a day?"

"Especially not for a day."

"Then let's just sit here on this bench until we can go back to the hotel."

"No, I'm too tired. It's probably going to be a long night. Explaining this day to Cuthbert is going to be hell on both of us. I want a little time to think."

He got up, wearily gesturing for her to walk ahead of him. He took the four o'clock position, and granted her no room for argument, for imperious command, or even for changing her mind.

She tore him up inside, but he had made his decision, as she had made hers.

He flagged a cab going north, and he directed the driver off the main streets into the residential blocks. They passed row after row of tidy brick bungalows and white frame split-levels.

On one corner, a cluster of children frolicked in

the geyser made by an open fire hydrant. Teens played a pickup basketball game on a fenced-in concrete court. The ice cream man waved to them from his truck.

"Tell me one last thing, Serena. Was it about my leaving the service? Because maybe I need to explain that."

"That's none of my business," she said, staring bleakly at the neighborhood.

"You're right, I guess. None of your business."

The cab stopped in front of a white Cape Cod style cottage with black shutters and a wide swath of red and white impatiens bordering the walkway. Dylan had scarcely paid the driver when the front door burst open.

"Dylan! Oh, my Dylan!"

A middle-aged woman wearing an oversize Hawaiian print shirt, black capris pants and pink flip-flops tore out of the house and flung herself into Dylan's arms.

"My baby's come home!" she wailed.

Serena bit back a smile at Dylan's obvious embarrassment mingled with equally obvious affection.

"Glad to be home, Ma."

His mother abruptly relinquished him. "You never told me you were coming into town," she accused. "I had to read about it in the latest issue of the *Weekly Star*."

Serena's eyes widened. "What did the article say about Dylan?"

Dylan's mother regarded Serena thoughtfully. "Just said that he had been hired to beef up security," she said, dropping her voice conspiratorially. "They had an old picture of him, when his hair was much shorter. Think I should send them a new one for their files?"

"Don't, Ma. I've had enough of them and their kind to last a lifetime," Dylan said. "Ma, this is Susan. She's the...uh, secretary to the princess. She's got the day off because the princess has the flu. And Susan, this is my mom."

Serena held out her right hand in the manner she had seen Americans use when they were going to shake.

"Now, Dylan," his mother said, jabbing a finger in her son's face. "The last time you lied to me was when you were eight years old and you said you fell off the monkey bars on the playground. I know for a fact that you and Rocco and Tony got bested by the neighborhood's equivalent to the James Gang."

"Yeah, so?"

"So I told you never to lie to me a second time," his mother said. "This is Her Royal Highness, the Princess Serena and I know it."

"Oh, no!" Serena cried out, mashing her fist into her mouth. "Is it that obvious who I am?" She glanced around the neighborhood. The girls playing hopscotch across the street didn't spare her a glance. But was that curtain on the second floor of the house next door moving suspiciously?

"You're only recognizable to a dedicated royal watcher like me," Mrs. MacPhail reassured her.

"You can count on my mom not to say anything," Dylan said tersely. "She's honorable."

"Your Royal Highness, my son's right. I'll never say a word to anyone. But I knew from the moment you got out of the cab."

"Oh, dear."

"You're in disguise but your kind of beauty can't be hidden. Nice haircut, by the way."

Serena opened her mouth, too shocked to even make the automatic good-mannered thank you.

"Dylan inherited his observation skills from me," Mrs. MacPhail continued. "I don't think most people would know you. Still, are we going to stand on the front lawn all afternoon waiting for one of the neighbors to ask themselves over for coffee?"

"No, of course not," Serena murmured.

"Besides, this is such a treat for me," the older woman said, linking her arm in Serena's. "Dylan's never brought home a girlfriend before."

Chapter Ten

"I've never met a princess before," Mrs. MacPhail said, drawing Serena into the living room. "Is it true that you can't wear purple to formal events because only the reigning monarch is allowed to wear royal colors?"

"Well, uh, actually..."

"How many rooms are there in the palace at the capital?"

"I only know what I've been told, but the figure is estimated at—"

"Do you really drink only carrot juice during the day to keep your figure?"

She patted the cushion next to her on the plaid upholstered couch.

"Ma, don't do this," Dylan warned, drawing the whispery soft lace curtains.

Softened-to-butter light shrouded the room. He picked up the telephone on the coffee table, listened for a second to the dial tone and hung up.

"Really, Dylan, I have an obligation as a guest

in your mother's house," Serena said. "Besides, these questions are not nearly as bad as the ones the press shouts at me every day. Mrs. MacPhail, true on purple, fourteen hundred rooms at latest count, and no, not at all. I don't even like carrots."

"Thought not," Mrs. MacPhail said, nodding sagely. "I gave it a try for two days last year and I haven't been able to look at a carrot since."

"But what I eat is regulated rather strictly."

"Yeah, but it seems to work." Mrs. MacPhail poked Serena's slender thigh. "But if I had to give up chocolate, it wouldn't be worth it. Do they at least let you have that?"

"Ma, please!" Dylan exclaimed. "This visit needs discretion. Are you having your bridge club ladies over this evening?"

She shot a "my son, such a worry wart" look at Serena.

"No, Dylan, bridge is tomorrow. Don't give me another thought, Your Highness. I've had many of Dylan's clients and friends in this living room, but I would go to an early grave rather than say a word about them," she said, placing a solemn hand over her heart. "Although my chicken fried steak has brought back one national leader so many times that I think the neighbors are catching on. It's hard to persuade your friends that your plumber does his business from a stretch limo with fifteen of Dylan's Secret Service agent buddies in tow."

"Mother!"

"All right, Dylan, what do you want?"

"I want you to go shopping."

"Mmm, I like that part. But why?"

"Because I'm asking. Please. Please go shopping."

"How long?"

"One hour," Dylan said, pulling a hundred-dollar bill from his wallet and laying it on the coffee table. "I need one hour, and wipe that look off your face. There's nothing between us. She needs some sleep and I need some downtime."

"So there's clean sheets in your room."

"We'll be in separate rooms. She'll take the guest room," he said. "I'll take my own room. Nothing, Mom, absolutely nothing's going on."

"Nothing?" Mrs. MacPhail asked, and Serena startled, thinking it had been her voice. Because Mrs. MacPhail's question was hers. Nothing? That kiss meant nothing? But, of course. He was a man of the world and for him, a kiss was…just a kiss.

For her it had been an awakening. An unwelcome awakening. A bittersweet knowledge of pleasures of which she would have been better off ignorant. She had put up the Do Not Touch sign, but she wished he would at least have some regrets and not simply regard their kiss as…

"Nothing," Dylan repeated.

"But, you look so good together!" Mrs. Mac-Phail wailed. "Besides, you're a Leo and she's a—"

"Nothing," Serena said, firmly shattering Mrs. MacPhail's illusions as surely as her own.

Mrs. MacPhail looked at Dylan, at Serena and then at her son again.

"You two are mighty foolish for being so smart. And I don't want your money, son."

"Think of it as an early Christmas present."

Mrs. MacPhail leaned forward to inspect the bill.

"This dead president would only last me twenty minutes," she speculated. "If I were to take him along."

He added two more bills.

"Thirty minutes, tops," his mom said.

He threw down two more. Five hundred dollars. "You always bargained hard with me," he groused amiably.

Mrs. MacPhail snapped up the money. "I'll be back in one hour," she said. "And I'm sorry to find out that you two aren't going to spend your time more productively. After all, you..."

"What, Ma? Are you crying?"

"No, I've got something in my eye. It's just...it's just you've both been through so much, you deserve some happiness in your lives. Even if it's only for an hour."

NOTHING.

The kiss was nothing.

She had bolted from Wrigley Field because she had thought their kiss meant something. Something she had never known before. Something that was worth everything. Something that was fiery hot and sweetly tender all at the same time. Something that would put her offtrack, something that could destroy all that she had put into place.

But Dylan had said it was just nothing. Although his scent lingered, the "nothing" man was down the hall.

"I'll put fresh sheets on the bed in the guest room for you," he had said.

"I'll help."

"Have you ever made a bed?"

"No."

"Then sit down," he ordered, shaking his head at her ignorance. "It'll take me less time to do it myself."

"Where are you going to stay?"

"In my old room. My mom keeps it the same as if I moved out yesterday. I'll be across the hall from you if you need anything."

Anything? She didn't need anything. It was nothing she wanted.

She felt an inexplicable sadness sweep through her—but why? She would sleep every night for the rest of her life alone. Why should an hour's much needed rest in a Chicago working-class neighborhood matter? Especially when it was what she wanted? Or, at least, what was best.

She sat back in the soft cushions of the living room couch, relinquishing the painfully strict regal posture that had been drilled into her at eighteen. She toyed with the idea of putting her feet on the coffee table.

Then decided that Mrs. MacPhail might not like that—although Dylan's mother looked to be the kind of woman who would put her feet wherever made her most comfortable. Serena settled for crossing her legs, and thought she could hear Lady Bostwick's tsk, tsk, tsk.

A princess might, in times of extreme casualness, cross her ankles but Serena's pose was positively…unprotocol.

A shaft of late afternoon sun highlighted the silvery dust motes floating in the air. The walls, clearly in need of a new coat of paint, had the warm patina of a crumbling Italian Renaisance palace. The love seat and matching chintz chair had scratched legs and subtle indentations in their cushions that indicated loving wear. The aubergine-and-spruce rug beneath her toes was so frayed and thin that it seemed to be made of a gossamer silk.

She imagined the room with children, her two sons and a girl. A baby girl, maybe two. Toys on the rug—if she were a commoner, she would be so happy that she wouldn't care about tidiness. Or, at least, not nearly as much as the keepers of the palace did.

Her boys had always left their sports equipment inside the front door—hockey sticks, skates, soccer balls, shin guards, cleats—infuriating the palace staff. But she never cared—that's the way boys are, she thought. She imagined a mug of steaming morning coffee, a vase of wildflowers...and a husband.

A real husband.

A husband who looked, in fantasy, surprisingly like Dylan.

Snap out of it! she warned herself.

She got up abruptly and went upstairs.

"I put on the sheets," Dylan said, coming out of a bedroom no bigger than the closet of the palace that housed her ball gowns. "And I got towels out in case you want to take a shower. I'll call Cuthbert at five o'clock and come wake you when it's time to go."

He walked across the hall to his own room, no longer inclined to linger, to talk, to listen. She had closed the door on him much earlier, when she had told him she wanted their day to end.

She sat on the bed, absently working a split seam on the quilt.

"Here, you probably don't even know how to pull back the sheets on a bed," he said, striding back in. He shooed her away, drew back the quilt to baby blue sheets. "Princess, lie down."

"I can't...I can't..."

"You have to," he urged. "You've been going since yesterday morning. The ball last night would have been enough to put most women to bed for a day and you're probably going to spend an equally grueling evening explaining this runaway thing to Cuthbert and Bostwick. Get some sleep.''

''I can't... I can't...''

''Hey, what's the matter?''

She looked up at him, his face swimming in the pool of her tears. She didn't mean to cry. Didn't mean to show any weakness. Had always figured she'd save all her tears, all the years and years worth of them, for when she was alone, really alone in the turrets of the ice-bound Isle of Whit's fortress.

''Oh, Princess,'' he said, shaking his head. ''Don't do this to me. I was always a sucker for a woman with a problem.''

He let his jacket drop to the floor and pulled the Glock out of his shoulder holster, automatically checking the safety before he put it carefully on the nightstand. Then he unbuckled his shoulder holster.

A thin bead of sweat ran along its shadow on his cotton T-shirt. He took off his belt and pulled his wallet out of his back pocket and put it on the nightstand next to his gun.

She watched all this with a vulnerable detachment. If he was seducing her, she had no will to stop him. In fact, there would be a certain relief that he would take responsibility. She could even imagine the afterward, when he would apologize for taking advantage of her. And she would be cloaked in a trustworthy anonymity. But a one-night stand was wrong. And it would be a one-night stand, even if it was only four o'clock in the afternoon.

He slipped off his shoes and she waited for him to take off his jeans.

He didn't.

She waited for his kiss.

He didn't kiss her.

She waited for him to pull her T-shirt over her head, to tug at the button of her jeans, to caress her swollen and aching breasts, to spread her trembling legs.

But he didn't.

Instead, he walked around the bed, pulled back the quilt and slipped between the sheets.

"Let's get some sleep, Princess," he said softly.

Sleep? No! He couldn't possibly mean sleep.

Brushing back her tears, she flipped her sneakers off. She got between the sheets, hoping that she wouldn't appear too inexperienced, too eager, too intense, too needy, too...too.

"No, that's not what we're going to do," he said, pulling her clumsy hand from the waistband of his jeans. "I'd like to. I really would. If I didn't think I'd explode in the process, I'd show you exactly how much. But this isn't what you need right now."

He rolled her over so that she faced away from him. A merciful act, since the seductive defeat hurt bad. And must show on her face.

He curled up behind her, his chest a strong support to her back, his legs molding to hers, his breath at her neck. He flopped an arm around her waist and held her tightly.

"This is what you need right now," he whispered. "This is what we both need."

His tenderness surprised her. Her need for it more.

"But I thought..."

"No, Princess, I'm not doing that. If you're looking for that, you'll have to go elsewhere. I can't."

"Why not? Is it me?"

"Not at all. But it's a long story. Too long for an hour."

"Tell me."

"No. I won't because I believe in taking advantage of a warm bed and rest when it's available," he said, the weariness cracking his voice. "But if you're still interested in an hour, I'll tell you the whole sorry tale."

She started to ask him again. And then knew he wouldn't budge.

Besides, his breath had stilled and his body seemed to settle into a peace—a peace that he brought, in spite of her, to each of them.

She would never go to sleep. She couldn't. It was too new, too exciting, too exotic to be wrapped in the luxury of this strong, virile man's arms. She wouldn't begrudge him his sleep, but she would memorize every detail of this closeness.

Wouldn't sleep.

Couldn't sleep.

Maybe she would just close her eyes.

Just for a minute.

The Field Museum Ball of the previous evening had been very long and she had been awake for...how many hours was it?

Chapter Eleven

She awoke to the smell of home cooking. Sweet, yet spiced with black pepper and just a touch of cinnamon.

The rumor about carrot juice hadn't been so far from the truth. Her clothes were made to her measurements to showcase the latest fashions and a drop or gain on the scale of a mere pound could spoil a designer's presentation of his work, and with that, a career. Her diet was managed with obsessive scientific precision by the palace.

Her mouth watered.

The room was dark and quiet, his side of the bed empty. She rolled over and luxuriated in the lingering warmth, the now familiar citrus-and-musk scent of him, the faintly bittersweet memory of his strong, sun-toasted arms around her.

She heard a voice from the hallway. She sprang to her feet and opened the door.

Rubbing sleep from her eyes, she was drawn to the light streaming from Dylan's boyhood room.

A teenaged boy's haven—trophies, ribbons and medals were draped and displayed on every available surface. His bed was covered with a red-and-black plaid wool blanket and books were shelved neatly over the desk.

Dylan stood facing the window, his jeans molded to his slender hips, a white towel slung over his naked shoulders. A thin rivulet of water ran between the lateral muscles of his back. His hair was wet and shiny and fell in waves at his shoulders. He had shaved, and his jaw looked as smooth as silk.

"Put me through to Cuthbert," he said. "Tell him it's MacPhail."

The floor creaked at her footstep.

He glanced back at her.

"Cuthbert, it's me."

She thought about returning to the Drake and onto her exile. Thought about the explanations and the recriminations and the tensions. She thought about the coming years of solitude. She felt unfinished, incomplete, her freedom for a day not enough. But, mostly, she felt obstinately sure of one thing: she didn't want to leave Dylan. Not yet.

She reached forward and touched his pale lips with her finger. She had made her decision, impulsive while still the culmination of a lifetime of denial.

He put his hand on the receiver. "Are you sure?" he whispered.

She nodded. Oh, yes, she was sure.

"Cuthbert, I'm sorry, man, I...I called to tell you...I lost her."

She smiled. From the phone, she could hear Cuthbert's shriek of outrage.

"I'm sorry," Dylan said. "I turned around and she was gone. But she can't get far. No...no...I know what I'm doing."

Oh, no, you don't, Serena thought. Neither of us knows what we're doing now.

Dylan spent the next few minutes in a charged but conciliatory conversation. Then he promised Cuthbert he'd bring Serena in by night's end.

He hung up the phone. "What do you want to do, Princess? My mother's downstairs cooking—she bought out Marshall Field's and came home in exactly an hour."

"Then I'll have what the president had," she said. "Chicken fried steak."

MRS. MACPHAIL FRETTED over a vase of blue-and-white delphinium as Dylan and Serena came downstairs. The round table at the center of the room was set with four gold-rimmed plates and sparkling crystal glasses.

It was only as Serena drew closer that she noticed the gold etching on the plates was faded and the soft white linen tablecloth hadn't been ironed. The silver plate flatware didn't match, but Serena was charmed by the pairings of unusual forks and whimsical spoons at each setting. The napkins were white waffle-weave kitchen towels with an inch-wide ribbon of cotton lace crocheted into the hem.

At the palace, a princess couldn't get even a simple midnight snack on such a table, but Serena felt oddly at home here. *Maybe I was meant to be a commoner,* she thought.

"Your sister's coming over," Mrs. MacPhail told Dylan. "And be nice to her—she's just coming off a long shift working a triple homicide."

"Your daughter is a police detective?" Serena asked.

"I never expected that, I can tell you," Mrs. MacPhail said, nodding ruefully. "She's five-two, pretty as a picture, had plenty of offers from modeling agencies even when she was just a kid."

"So she was going to be a model?" Serena asked.

"No. She was destined to be a dancer. Could kick her feet over her head when she was five. I must have spent every minute I wasn't working driving her from one lesson to another—ballet, tap, flamenco, Irish step. And Dylan can tell you that every spare penny we had from his job went to paying for lessons."

"But she couldn't get work dancing?"

"Oh, no, she had a job lined up in New York with a dance company to start the day after she graduated from the local junior college."

"So I'm very confused. What happened?"

"Her brother here had just gotten a job at Secret Service," she said, glancing back at Dylan, who leaned against the doorjamb. "He was working a detail for a presidential candidate campaigning in the city that spring and she begged him to let her tag along."

"And?"

"And the next thing I knew, she wanted a different kind of life and was training for the policeman's physical exam. By August, I was ironing the dress blues and gave away her leotards to cousins."

"Oh, Mrs. MacPhail! You must have been very upset," Serena empathized. "Why didn't you just tell her that she would have to take the job as a dancer?"

"Why would I do that? She's happy doing what she's doing. Sure, I was upset for a while. But that passed pretty quickly."

"But she was given the talent for dancing...."

"Oh, that. Yeah, I rib her a lot about wanting back pay on all the car pooling I did. But I'm not serious. Your kids have to choose their own lives—and if she's found what makes her happy, then I'm happy. Who knows? Maybe your sons will decide that instead of princes they'd like to be doctors or lawyers or carpenters."

Serena shook her head emphatically. Mrs. MacPhail was a charming woman, a wonderful woman, but she didn't understand the fact that being born to nobility gave a person no choices.

"My sons couldn't possibly do anything other than what they are born to do."

"Ma," Dylan warned.

"What'd I say? You're about to tell me I'm saying somethin' wrong. It's like the time I talked to the president about our policy on human rights in China. I sez to him—"

"Ma, don't you think dinner's burning?"

"Oh, my goodness. You're right. If those steaks get overdone, I'll have to send you out to the grocery store for more. Charlotte's gotta have protein in her diet if she's going to chase after the criminal element."

Mrs. MacPhail disappeared into the kitchen.

"Sorry about my mom," Dylan said, sitting across from Serena. "She speaks her mind. But sometimes she shouldn't."

"I think she's great," Serena said truthfully. "And I suppose it would be interesting what my boys would choose for their lives if they weren't who they are."

"Any conclusions?"

"I think Erik might be a businessman. And Vlad might do something with computers," Serena said. "But I'm sure those would be their second choices. They are leaders of a country first."

"But a mother can be wrong. Look at my sister Charlotte."

"Yeah, look at me," said a lilting, feminine voice.

"Hey, lieutenant!" Dylan said easily, standing up

to hug the diminutive, casually dressed redhead who walked in from the front porch. "How's business?"

"Too good," Charlotte said, holding her hand out to Serena. "I'm in the line of work that you hope experiences serious downsizing. You must be Dylan's girlfriend."

"Actually, I'm...Serena."

They shook hands and Serena didn't even feel odd about the physical contact. Maybe she was getting used to being a commoner.

"Serena. Nice name. Just like the... Hey, aren't you the princess herself?"

"Yes, she is," Dylan said. "But not a word outside of the family."

"That's cool," Charlotte said, pulling off her blazer and tugging at the shoulder holster that held her regulation pistol. "I signed a get well card to you from the precinct. I take it you're not sick, you're just playing hooky?"

"Something like that."

"Everybody needs to once in a while. Hey, you changed your hair. It's cute. Does it take a lot of upkeep?"

Serena reached up to the wisps of hair.

"Just a pair of scissors."

"Better get your hair cut now," Dylan advised, tugging on his sister's long, thick ponytail. "Because this is going to be the hottest style."

"If it looks as good on everybody as it does on

you, Serena, he's probably right. Where's Mom, by the way?''

"Making dinner."

"All right, good to meet you, Serena. Are you stayin' for dinner? Must be—Mom's put out all the best china. You know what that means, Dylan.''

"Uh-huh. I call dibs on drying."

"No way. You got drying the last time that rock star was here. You get clearing the table. I get drying. And she—" Charlotte pointed to Serena "—she gets washing.''

"You can't give her a job. She's a princess."

Serena laughed. "That's all right, Dylan. Your sister's absolutely right. I'm playing hooky. I'm not a princess for today. I'd be happy to wash dishes.''

Charlotte smirked triumphantly at her brother.

"See? She's cool."

"That's the highest praise Charlotte gives to a person,'' Dylan said as his sister went into the kitchen. "And don't worry. Nobody'll really make you wash dishes.''

"But I'd like to," Serena said. "You don't understand, do you? I feel like I could do everything. Everything that a normal woman would do. And that includes dishes.''

He took her measure. "What made you change your mind about going in? Cuthbert had his plans in place, I'm sure. We could have had you back at the Drake within the hour.''

"I...I'm not sure," she said.

It was difficult to explain, and made impossible when she looked up into his deep blue eyes. She had felt something like safety lying in bed in his arms, something like trust, something like happiness, something like...

Something like love, but surely not real.

Whatever it was, she wasn't quite ready to give it up, even as the most reasonable side of her insisted it was time to go.

She could never explain all this to him, when she barely understood it herself.

"Do you mind that I'm staying?"

"Mind? Not at all. Just...baffled."

She was grateful that Dylan's mother chose that moment to call for her son to make the salad.

"As long as you're in the mood for being a commoner—" Dylan said, shaking a playfully stern finger in her face "—you can peel potatoes."

ON THE OTHER SIDE of the city, on the penultimate floor of the Drake Hotel, Cuthbert put the phone down and rubbed his fleshy palms together.

"How'd I do?"

The young suit sitting at the desk pulled off his headphones.

"I'm sorry, sir. You didn't keep him on long enough. I wasn't able to get a certain fix on his location. Can't you just get a phone number from him? It would help immeasurably."

"I don't think you quite understand the point,"

Cuthbert said witheringly. "We're not trying to pin-point his location. Yet."

"Then what is the point?" asked one of the two agents sitting on the couch.

The other agent sitting beside him paused his pocket video game so that he could look up at his boss.

"Sorry, sir. I don't understand, either. What exactly is the point?"

Cuthbert stared heavenward and counted to ten—make that twenty. "The point is to save the throne. And our country," he explained, wondering how he had unearthed such insufferable idiots. "And to do that we must destroy her. Utterly destroy her."

Chapter Twelve

The MacPhail kitchen was large by the standards of the neighborhood. Mrs. MacPhail explained that Dylan had paid for a major expansion when she took up cooking classes as a hobby upon her retirement from the factory.

Still, even with a lot of space, two butcher block workstations and a double refrigerator, the atmosphere in the kitchen was cozy and crowded.

Humming along to the country music playing on her radio, Mrs. MacPhail fussed over the steaks hissing in the frying pan. Dylan showed Serena how to peel and slice the potatoes but shooed her away when it became clear that she couldn't do anything with her hands.

"You're going to cut yourself," Dylan said.

"Give me something else to do."

"All right, you butter the bread. Does this mean you're making the salad?" he asked his sister.

"No, I'm in charge of dessert."

"And what are you making?"

"Apple pie."

"Get out!" Dylan cried. "You can't bake a pie."

Charlotte looked wounded.

"I picked it out myself," she said. "And that's as close as I get to domestic stuff."

Munching on some celery, she entertained them with a convoluted story of office politics down at the precinct house. It was clear she enjoyed her work, even as she groused about the inefficiencies of Chicago's police bureaucracy.

When they sat for dinner, Mrs. MacPhail asked her son to say a short grace, which he did.

"Oh, I'm so happy to have my children here!" Mrs. MacPhail said, squeezing Serena's hand as Dylan said amen. "You can't imagine how seldom I get both of them at the same table. Well, maybe you do. You have two boys getting up there in years. I bet you miss them."

"I do," Serena said. "They grew up way too fast for me."

"Way too fast," Mrs. MacPhail agreed.

Over the simple American cuisine, talk turned to the life of the princess. The MacPhail women seemed to instinctively understand what questions were trivial enough to answer and which were just too sensitive to reply to. Serena told them about her childhood in the country palace which had belonged to her family since the Dark Ages—and looked as if it had been decorated by Viking barbarians. For

Mrs. MacPhail's benefit, she described the palace rooms.

"You would love the ballroom," she assured Charlotte. "It's larger than your American football fields and it's covered with a marble parquet—but perhaps you don't dance any longer."

"Oh, I dance," Charlotte said. "But I do it for fun now. I can enjoy it more when I'm not worrying about how I'm doing at it."

As Charlotte cut the apple pie, Serena related several amusing anecdotes about her early years at court. She even explained the truth behind a much reported incident from her eldest son's childhood in which he threw a bucket of water from a turret onto the heads of the ceremonial guards. Mrs. MacPhail laughed so hard that tears sprang to her eyes.

"He sounds like quite a prankster," Charlotte observed. "Almost as bad as Dylan."

"Oh, really?" Serena said. "And just what are some of the things that he did that are as bad as what I just told you about my son?"

Charlotte opened her mouth, relishing the chance to get back at her older brother.

"Don't you dare say a word, Charlotte," Dylan warned, playfully menacing her with his butter knife. "If you tell her anything, I can retaliate with a few tales from your sordid past."

"Ha! I dare you to top this one. You see, Dylan was ten years old. I was just six. And..."

As Charlotte launched into a convoluted story featuring chicanery, hijinx and a healthy dose of sibling rivalry, Serena found herself wishing the boys were here.

How they'd enjoy themselves in this atmosphere that was so much warmer than the silence and formality of dinner at the palace hall!

How they would thrive in the warm glow of love and acceptance that ran through this house!

She felt a sudden stab of longing to speak with them, to see them here, right now. They had grown up so quickly and in a few more short years would be adults with their own duties and responsibilities. Their own lives intertwined with the country's future. She missed them so much when she took these trips and she knew that she'd miss them even more when she was in her exile.

Dylan must have noticed her mercurial change of emotion, because he reached over to squeeze her hand just as she found the depth of her despair.

"You all right?" he whispered.

"Fine," she lied.

He left his hand where it was and she didn't pull away. Instead, she drew strength and calmness from him, reasoning that she would soon see her boys, that they probably didn't miss her nearly as much as she did them—which was entirely normal for teenaged boys—and that she couldn't call them now because the palace was most certain to trace her phone call.

Besides, she had not, even during the darkest mo-

ments of her marriage, allowed her sons to be forced
to choose one side or another, to favor their mother
or their father. And contacting them now would certainly put them in that position.

Mrs. MacPhail glanced over, saw her son's fingers entwined with Serena's and looked away
quickly. Her thoughts may have been momentarily
somber, but the glowing warmth of the MacPhail
dining room worked its magic.

Serena concentrated on understanding the de-
nouement of Charlotte's tale, which involved great
injury to her at the hands of her brother.

"Yeah, right," Dylan balked. "That's not how it
happened at all."

He retaliated with a grievance of his own, an an-
ecdote from years past that he related with gusto.
Serena suspected the tales of their youth had become
embellished with each retelling, but they were nonetheless enjoyable.

As the summer sun fell at last to night, Charlotte
announced she had to go back to her own apartment
to change her clothes for a date. Mrs. MacPhail
looked at her watch.

"Heavens! I'm going to be late for bingo if I
don't hurry. Charlotte, will you drive?"

"Sure, Ma. Sorry, brother dearest," Charlotte
said as she picked up her holster. She strapped it
around her waist. "I guess this means you'll be pulling double duty in the kitchen."

"And when has it been any different?"

"Gimme a break. I'm driving Mom," she said. "I don't know why she gets such a kick out of riding in an unmarked police car. Most nights, she makes me put the cherries on the roof and rev the siren when we back out of the driveway."

Serena started stacking dishes to take them into the kitchen. Mrs. MacPhail put a hand on her shoulder.

"It's okay, I really want to do dishes," Serena said.

"Oh, no, I'm not stopping you. I would never stop anybody who wanted to do housekeeping in my home!" Mrs. MacPhail said. "And if you feel a great longing to do the floors, have Dylan bring the vacuum out." She laughed. "No, I just wanted to say goodbye. I'd imagine you have important places to go to and people to see. You probably won't be here when I get back. And I want you to know how much it meant to me to meet you, how much I hope you find the happiness in life that you deserve." She drew Serena into a bear hug.

Serena didn't stiffen, as she ordinarily did on the rare occasions when a fan would break from the crowd and rush to touch her. Instead, she did the unthinkable. She hugged back.

"Be kind to my son," Mrs. MacPhail warned. "He doesn't show his feelings, but as his mom, I know him well. He's a good man, honest and loyal and strong. Please don't break his heart too badly."

"Mrs. MacPhail, I'm not..."

Dylan's mom pulled away from the embrace and faked as if to swoon.

"I've actually met a princess," she said loudly. "Only thing is, I can't tell anybody about it."

"That's all right, Ma," Charlotte said. "We can talk about it in the car. You can tell me everything and I'll pretend I'm hearing it for the first time. Nice meeting you, Your Highness."

"Please, it's just Serena."

"Well, goodbye, Serena."

The two women left and the house fell so quiet that Serena heard the refrigerator hum and the shouts of children playing basketball in the alley. She picked up the dishes from the table and carried them in to Dylan, who had rolled up his sleeves and plunged his arms up to his biceps in dishwater.

"Want some music?" she asked.

"Sure."

She flipped on the radio and was carried into the rhythm of working. She knew she'd look back on this as one of the highlights of her day.

Just as the last glass was polished to a sparkling clarity and placed in the honey pine cabinet, they heard a quiet knock on the front door.

Serena startled. Dylan pressed his finger to her lips and motioned her up the stairs.

"What if it's Cuthbert?"

"Trust me, I'll take care of it," he replied.

He didn't tell her that something about Cuthbert's complacency had troubled him. Was it possible that

Cuthbert had been tailing them all along, waiting for the moment when Dylan and Serena were alone? The scandal would destroy them both.

He patted his shoulder holster, just checking. As she tiptoed to the top of the landing he wondered if he should have sent her out the back door. But if Cuthbert was only half as smart as he claimed to be, he would have his men covering the back.

Dylan took a deep breath, tried for nonchalance and settled for a wary grimace. He opened the door to find three neighborhood children dressed in shorts and dirt-smudged T-shirts. Rocco's two nephews and Eddie's cousin's youngest boy.

Dylan released a weary sigh, and felt a relieved grin spread across his face. He shook his head.

"What do you fellas want?"

"Hey, Dylan, can you shoot a few hoops?" Tommy asked, his voice as gruff as his uncle's.

"Yeah, show us that slam dunk thing," his brother Ryan added.

Dylan opened the screen door. "All right, but you gotta let my friend play."

"Is he any good?" Tommy challenged.

"It's a she."

"You have a girlfriend? Yuck!"

"I'm not playing basketball with no girl," Tommy said, shaking his hands in front of him in an effort to fend off the ridiculous notion.

"Then sorry, boys, I can't play," Dylan said, starting to close the door.

"All right, all right," the boys agreed. "But she better be good."

"Serena! I mean, Susan!" Dylan called. "It's all right. You can come downstairs!" when no response came he said to the boys, "Oh, hold on. Wait here."

He found her cowering by the stairwell.

"It's just some neighborhood kids. When they know I'm home, they want to play a little pickup game."

"Pickup?"

"Basketball. Didn't Bostwick give you a hundred-page report on it?"

"Actually, no."

"You wanna try anyhow?"

Her face brightened.

"Yeah, I would."

She followed him out to the front porch. Tommy, Ryan and Eddie's cousin gave her the once-over.

"You know anything at all about basketball?" Ryan asked.

"Not really," Serena admitted.

Tommy looked up at Dylan. "Do we have to take her?"

"Yes," Dylan said firmly.

They walked down to the corner playground and Dylan quickly outlined the rules for Serena. But before they could divide into teams, two more neighborhood kids came out to play. Within minutes, they had two full squads.

It was a good game and Dylan modulated his play so that half hour later it was a tie.

"I'm beat!" he complained, bending over as if he were struggling for breath. "I can't go over-time."

"Ice cream?" asked one young player.

Dylan looked up at Serena. "I always take the gang out for a treat afterward," he told her, adding a quick apology.

"Good, take me too," Serena said.

As they walked down the street to the Ice Cream Shoppe, several moms waved from their front porches, warning their children to come back soon—and remember to thank Dylan for the ice cream! A group of men on a front stoop waved at Dylan as he led the children's parade.

AFTER A QUICK SHOWER, Dylan pulled a collection of records from a stack in the living room.

"Records? I didn't know anyone still used re-cords," Serena said, crouching down next to him to look at the album covers. "I thought everything was on CD."

"Not this stuff," he said. "These are the classics. Ah, here's my favorite. Ma forgot to tell you that I did a lot of the driving to take Charlotte to her les-sons. Care to dance?"

He placed a record on the spindle.

"Dance? You mean, with you? Here?"

"Yeah, you said you wanted to dance."

"I do."

"I heard the aides talking about how difficult it is to find a dance partner for you at these fancy dos," he said, holding his hand out to her. "He must be taller than you."

"Hard to manage because I'm five-eight in stockings," she said.

They stood. He was at least six inches taller than she was. She ignored the tremor of her legs. He took her right hand in his firm grip. The record dropped to the turntable and began to play a scratchy tango.

"Must be married," he continued, staring deep into her eyes.

"And the marriage must be strong," she agreed. "Without a hint of scandal. Wife to give press interviews gushing with delight at the honor of having her husband dance with me, the princess."

"He must be photogenic."

"But not movie star handsome," she added.

"Captain of industry," he murmured, sliding his other arm around her waist.

"But a doctor or head of a charity will do nicely. Or the head of the armed forces of a country which is allied with our nation."

"Can't spend more than three minutes in his arms," he said. He spun her around the living room and then two-two-three-four, his thigh lightly grazed her legs.

"And definitely, most definitely," Serena concluded, "he can't be fun."

"Sorry I couldn't find you a proper dance partner, Princess."

"Oh, I think you'll do for tonight."

Chapter Thirteen

Outside, a mother called her children in for bedtime. From far away, a car alarm squealed and then went silent. A popular song wailed from a boom box. Streetlights blinked on, casting a tranquil amber glow throughout the street.

The MacPhail's living room was neat and tidy, clearly maintained with care and love. But it wasn't a sprawling ballroom. It was a living room without the slightest regal pretension.

This was no gala affair, no glittering party, no swanky evening.

Dancing in Dylan's arms didn't have any of the trappings of elegance and taste that Serena had been reared to expect as both her due and her duty. But it was the dance that she would always remember as her finest.

Dylan held her close to him, forgetting the strictness of propriety, forgetting the risks, forgetting the consequences, forgetting himself.

He murmured the last strains of the sentimental

tune, his breath caressing her earlobe. He gently guided her with a hand at the small of her back, navigating the tight spaces between the love seat and the chair, the magazine rack and the coffee table.

Though she had initially maintained the minimally proper three inches between them, it quickly became apparent that Dylan didn't dance by the rules—or even by the lessons from his youth.

He danced by instinct. And his instinct was all male.

And her response was all woman.

When his leg brushed against hers, it was no accident and yet there was no guile.

She wanted him, wanted him to kiss her again, even—shocking herself—wanted him inside her, wanted him to bring to completion the coiled, throbbing nub of her excitement. Her breasts grazed his chest and instead of backing off in flustered modesty, she reveled at the aching fullness that she felt. She noted the responsive tensing of his groin.

What had he said? Only heterosexual male on earth without any interest in sleeping with her?

His hand drifted from the demure concave of her back to the gentle swelling curve of her hips and she did not protest, but teased him by pressing against the manhood that strained against his jeans.

As he lost the thread of the final song, she raised her head to him, offering her parted lips. But his expression was one of agony, not the expected delight.

"Princess, do you know what you're doing to me?" he groaned.

"I know exactly what I'm doing," she lied.

She stood on her tiptoes and decided the course of their fates with a petal soft brush of her lips against his.

There are a thousand different kinds of kisses—from the oh-so-continental kiss on the hand to the air kiss of jet-set acquaintances to a lover's consummation kiss.

But this was Dylan's kiss. His mouth caught hers just as her teasing sweep against his flesh was nearly over. He brought her to him, tensing as he reined his strength, his power and her surrender. And he took control of her, his firm lips bringing them both to the brink of pleasure.

She felt a purring sound vibrating at her throat. More, she wanted more. So much more.

Suddenly, she knew the truth about herself. She had wanted on this day to experience everything a normal woman would, but it hadn't been seeing the animals at a zoo or rooting for a baseball team or eating waffles that had driven her to seek her freedom.

No, she had wanted this.

In some part of her that she had not—to this very moment—acknowledged, she had wanted this.

And now, she could have it.

It seemed all she had to do was ask.

But she couldn't.

He relinquished her.

"You don't know what you're asking for," he said harshly.

"It's you I want, Dylan."

"I could be any man," he cut her off. "You could have your pick. Your pledge of celibacy and your country's history of beheading its princesses be damned. You could choose any man. It's not me you want."

"I could have any man," she conceded, knowing that her status as a princess and a celebrity made the statement one of fact and not of pride. "I could have any man. But I don't want any man. I want you. Please…please, Dylan, don't make me beg."

He softened, raising his hand from the small of her back, touching her hair in mingled wonder and despair.

"You don't know who I am," he said. "You don't know what this will cost you."

She stiffened.

"Not me," he said. "I won't be the one extracting a price for this."

"Then I know enough for tonight. And tonight's all we've got."

"No, there's some things I should tell you. Things you have a right to know. Things that will make you change your mind."

He strode across the room and flipped off the record player.

Serena shivered, though there was no cold.

"Okay, I'm listening," she said, the rush of terrible premonition turning her legs to jelly. She sat on the couch.

"You know I worked for the Secret Service," Dylan said, turning around but coming no closer. "And I left last year. The president did not ask for my resignation, although the pressure from many quarters was mounting. I left because I felt I could no longer do my job effectively. For me, that was failure. Everything that I had built up—a career, a sense of who I am, my life—had been destroyed because I made a mistake."

She waited for him to go on, knowing that if he just came to her, put his arms around her, let her run her hands through his hair—if he made contact with her—she could be strong.

But he stood across the room, virtual miles between them.

"I compromised my position as an agent."

"In what way?"

"A political enemy of the president got damaging information about his fund-raising practices. From a file that was entrusted to me."

"Damaging information?" she asked flatly.

"Yes. It could have cost him the election."

"Is this what your friends were talking about this afternoon?"

"Yes."

"Why did you do it?"

"It was a woman. She was an aide to the Speaker

of the House. She came to me with a story—that her father had died and that she needed comfort. That she knew that my own father had died and she thought I would be in a special position to empathize with her. We had always been attracted to each other...or maybe I always misread her signals. But she wanted to do a little more than cry on my shoulder," he added wryly. "It was more effective than a straightforward come-on line. Because a straightforward come-on line I would have refused—because the rules didn't allow for an agent in my position to be with her. But I've always had a weakness for a damsel in distress."

"Let me guess—there was no dead father."

"No, it turned out he's a retired steelworker. As healthy as a horse."

"And the comforting?"

He ducked his head, too embarrassed or maybe too honorable to say anything more.

"Afterward, she went through my desk and through my papers while I lay sleeping. She found what she had been looking for and the Speaker of the House had a field day. I made a mistake having her at my apartment, not remembering to lock up the documents that I was entrusted with by the president. Even though he forgave me, I couldn't forgive myself. And my reputation was ruined. Utterly ruined. I had to resign."

"Why are you telling me this?"

"Because I'm trying to tell you that one night

carries risks. Sometimes the risks are too great. I've had to fight a reputation as a gigolo, as a man who can't control himself, a man with a weakness for women, a man who could and did compromise the trust of those he's sworn to serve. If it happens a second time, even my staunchest supporters will question my judgment. And Princess, be honest. You can't afford the damage of one night, either.''

"You're an honorable man," she said, thinking about all she knew of him. "You won't hurt me."

"I want to be honorable. I try to be. But I've made mistakes. Misjudgments. And maybe I do have a weakness for a woman in need."

"Is that what I am to you—a woman in need? A charity case? Someone to pity?"

"No, forgive me, but I don't want to comfort you, I don't want to pity you, I don't want you crying on my shoulder. I want to take you into my bed and make love to you all night long."

She rose to her feet and walked to him. Without waiting for his permission, she let her hand drop to the bulging hardness that strained against his jeans.

She didn't know what she was doing.

She would never have thought herself possessed of the courage or brazenness or both that was required for a woman to touch a man that way.

She didn't know if she was being seductive, acting foolish, making him more excited or committing the equivalent of throwing him into a cold shower.

But she acted on instinct, an instinct long suppressed.

"Dylan, I trust you. And for me, this is worth it."

There it was, a low growl that came from deep within him. His eyes were hooded and darkened with pleasure.

She felt her triumph welling in her chest.

And then he gripped her arms firmly, pushing her away from him.

"Dylan, wha—?"

"Not here," he said. "Please, not here."

All she desired was slipping through her fingers. She frantically grasped at her rationales.

"But we're alone. Your mother's not here. She's at bingo."

"She'll be back in an hour."

"So! That's an hour. An hour more than I've had all my life."

"Serena, I'm not the kind of stud who can perform on command."

"I didn't mean it to sound like that."

"Princess, what I want to do with you is going to take us all night. It's not a one-hour thing."

She looked up at him, wondering if her quickened heartbeat was fear, anticipation or both.

THIS IS WRONG, he thought as he pulled the car out into traffic. The blue Camaro sedan was his nineteenth birthday present to himself, bought with the first money he had earned that hadn't gone for the mortgage on his mother's house, Charlotte's braces or to the monthly tab from the corner grocery store. For years, he had stored it in his mother's garage and was now gratified to discover that his mother always kept it filled with gas.

The pleasure of the drive, reconnecting with a piece of his personal history, was overshadowed by his second thoughts. He was taking advantage of Serena's vulnerability, wasn't he?

He should give her a chaste peck on the cheek and take her straight back to the Drake.

But another chaste peck on the cheek would lead right back to the kind of passionate trouble that was sending them out into the starry summer night.

Like any professional in his business, he had a safe house. No one knew of its existence. Or where it was. Although the safety deposit box he had rented for his mother and Charlotte had the key and detailed directions to its location in an envelope to be opened in the event something dire happened to him.

He had never entertained a guest there. Never had any mail sent to him. Guarded like a priceless treasure the unlisted number that ran to the single telephone in the kitchen. He had never even heard the ring of that phone. No one knew it existed.

He followed the side streets out to the expressway and headed north. He had told her an hour and a half, but when he saw the sparse traffic, he knew they would reach the Wisconsin border town in slightly less than an hour.

The time seemed like an eternity.

With any other woman, he might have rented a hotel room. Or suggested they go to her place. Or even taken her to the Gold Coast loft that served as his office—it had a wood-burning stove, a fully stocked wine cabinet, and a king-size bed covered with Porthault sheets.

He would have made love once in quick and forceful passion and then again in lazy and contented sensuality. As for the third time...

But Serena wasn't any other woman. She was a princess on the run. A hotel room wasn't going to be her style. Her own place was a fourteen-hundred-room palace half a world away.

And his office was the first place Cuthbert would deploy his men if he doubted Dylan's story.

And he should be suspicious.

Dylan had called him from his cell phone from his mother's tiger lily garden.

The grumbling head of security for the princess had made Dylan run through the details of his "leads" twice but professed great enthusiasm for Dylan's talents at tracking. The words of praise were strangely grating.

"I've reviewed the clippings in the background file the palace sent me," Cuthbert had said. "When I read over how you managed to track down that billionaire's son's kidnappers, I was once again impressed. Top job, old boy. You really are the best at what you do. Just bring the princess in.''

With a promise to do just that, Dylan had taken the car out of the garage, leaving a note on the kitchen table explaining its absence to his mother. His mother would know well enough that Dylan never explained his own comings and goings, but taking his precious car was different.

On the expressway, Serena said nothing. She stared straight ahead, face illuminated by the southbound traffic headlights, looking like a woman being driven to her execution. She was scared. Scared of what she was risking. Scared of what she was doing. Scared of herself. Scared of him.

This is wrong, he chastised himself again. For being in her midthirties, she was still in so many ways a much younger woman, almost a girl. She was risking everything for one night of pleasure and she was so inexperienced that she wouldn't know that one night never satisfies and so often stings.

He should know.

But she trusted him. And that trust made his heart swell and his reason get tossed out the window.

''When I was young,'' he said, ''women came my way. It never seemed to be a problem finding one who wanted to make love and I was driven by my appetites and not by my brains.''

''Are you telling me you have a health problem?''

''No, no, nothing like that.''

''Are you bragging?'' she asked solemnly.

"Hardly. In fact, I'm rather ashamed of how I lived. I was just trying to tell you that one-night stands very seldom turn out well. Even if your partner is not acting as a spy."

"Then I have to trust you."

"Yes, I think so," he said.

"Dylan, I don't want anything more than tonight. We can't have anything more than tonight. I don't know why I want you so much, or why I'm acting so wantonly," she waved away his sputtered protest that she was no wanton. "All I know is that you're giving me a gift that I'll cherish for a lifetime."

Chapter Fourteen

He pulled off the exit at Kenosha, just north of the Wisconsin border. Going west, away from the lake, the ribbon of road passed through dairy farms and wooded hills and towns so small they were gone in a blink of an eye. Towns with only one stoplight. Towns with redbrick one-room schools. Towns where a couple could lose themselves for a night.

The four-lane county highway became a two-lane street and finally narrowed to a gravel-covered lane.

They were shrouded in the deepest of night, above them only a scant sliver of moon, no streetlights and just occasionally did they pass a house sporting a solitary light in a second-story window.

Nonetheless, Dylan switched off the headlights as they turned onto an unmarked dirt path. He scanned the rearview mirror several times and rolled down his window to listen past the whining cicadas and the crackle of cornstalks falling under the car's tires.

Then he tapped the accelerator, and the car lurched forward through the field.

"What's the matter?"

"Nothing to worry about. I don't want anyone following us," Dylan replied. "It's the way I've been trained. It's how I do things. I probably couldn't park in a grocery store parking lot without checking."

"Have we been followed?"

He considered telling her the truth. That he didn't know. That he couldn't be sure. That he had an uneasy feeling, call it a professional hunch, but there was nothing he could put his finger on.

Every time he had flipped the rearview mirror to study the cars in back of them on the highway, he had shook his head. Nothing.

Every time he stopped to pay a toll, he looked around and discovered nothing.

He had even doubled back once on the frontage road and found nothing.

He couldn't be sure.

It bothered him, because that was what he had been good at. Being sure. Maybe he had lost his touch.

Because she had so jangled his nerves and played with his heart and senses that he couldn't accurately judge whether he was doing a good job or a passable job or even a disastrous one.

Sometimes he had gotten the same feeling in the Service, when he had pulled long, unbroken shifts, when lack of sleep would finally take his reason.

He would work by instinct then.

And he worked by instinct now.

But raw instinct was the poorest substitute for good judgment.

"Relax, we're not being followed," he said with more confidence than he felt. "Forgive me, Princess, but it's in my nature to check out the cars around me, drop back on my route, generally take precautions."

"I'm glad you do. Thank you."

"No problem," he said.

"Have you ever had a woman here?"

"No one, Serena," he said. "No one has ever been here. Not even Charlotte or my mother."

"Why not?

"I have my privacy to hang on to, just as you do. The only person who even knows this house is here is the kid from the next farm over. I pay him to mow the lawn every week in the summer, clean the gutters in the fall and sweep the snow from the steps in winter."

The corn pressed against the car, stalks swiping against the windows and crackling beneath the tires. Just when Serena thought she might succumb to claustrophobia, Dylan flipped on the headlights and brought the car out into a grassy clearing.

Motion sensitive lights scattered through the yard illuminated a white farmhouse with a wraparound porch, black shutters and cherry red flowers in its window boxes. A solemn oak tree stood guard.

"Home," Dylan said.

He reached across her lap and flipped open the passenger door. The air was damp and smelled green with summer.

"Princess, one thing before we go inside," he said. "You are in the middle of nowhere with a man you don't know too well and there isn't a single other person on earth who knows where you are."

"Are you trying to scare me?"

"No. I'm trying to explain that you're safer than you would be in your own palace. If you don't want to do something, you tell me. If you want to spend the night playing a board game or watching television or just sitting around and talking, that's fine with me. It's whatever you want. Tonight is for you."

"Later," she said. "I might want all those things later."

She got out of the car, following him up the steps to the front door.

She wasn't sure what she expected. She knew men didn't ordinarily decorate their lairs with all the touches that make a house a home. But when he flicked on the lights in the living room and slipped past her into the next room, she stood awestruck.

The living room was furnished with a moss-colored chenille sofa and two apricot velvet club chairs that looked as comfortable as clouds. The honeyed pine coffee table was stacked with newspapers, magazines and heavy books. An intricately patterned quilt hung on the wall at the far end of the room and a rustic wood panel advertising a brand of horse hoof balm leaned on the mantel over the redbrick fireplace.

Beyond the dining room door, Serena saw a pine hutch, a long dark wood table with matching benches and a chandelier that had been fashioned from a verdigris copper weather vane.

"Want a drink?" Dylan asked, coming in from the kitchen. "All I've got is root beer, but it's nice and cold and brewed in the nearest town."

She took the glass he held out.

"Every one around here drinks from jelly jars," he explained. "It's kinda like that crystal your country's famous for."

"Well, then, cheers," she said, clinking her jar against his. She sipped self-consciously and then savored the brew. It was, as promised, icy cold. And its taste dark and spicy and sweet.

"Let's go look at the stars," Dylan said. "On a night like this, with not much of a moon, you can see millions and millions of them."

She shook her head, darting a glance at the stairway that ran up from a corner of the dining room.

"Dylan, I thought we would, uh…"

She wondered if she was making a mistake being so bold with him, and worse, losing what shred of dignity she possessed.

"Ah, Princess, you must feel that you have to cram a whole lifetime into this night."

"But I do."

"No, darlin', you're young, you've got years ahead of you," he said, ignoring Serena's grimace. "And every one of those years can count for something. Even on the Island of Whit. Besides, it's only trained seals and seventeen-year-old boys who can perform on command. What we're going to do is going to last a little longer. I need a little romancin'."

Dragging a quilt from the honeyed pine armoire which stood by the front door, he guided her to the backyard of the house.

"Here, sit down, no, don't go any farther, you'll fall right into the lake."

She peered down into darkness, illuminated only by the single bulb on the back porch light. Sure enough, the rich fresh smell of water. And a lap, lap, lap of gentle waves.

Letting her eyes adjust to the darkness, she looked across the waters to the horizon dotted with pine trees.

"Lake Michigan?" she asked. "That must be Canada over there."

"No, Lake Michigan's east of here. This is Lake...Lake Serena."

She looked at him sharply. His face was in the shadow and she couldn't tell if he was teasing her.

"It's my lake," he said, shrugging. "I own all the land you can see, and if it weren't for night there's a lot to see. I've never named the lake, but Serena has a pretty ring to it."

She faced the dark water. "I've had a fighter jet and a cruise missile loading dock christened Serena, but a lake?" she mused. "I think I like this a lot. Lake Serena."

"Look up. There's more. Much more."

The stars were like a scattering of diamonds on black velvet.

"I've never seen so many."

"I hadn't either 'til I bought this place. I'm a city boy and you've spent a lot of time cooped up in a palace. Too much man-made light."

He pointed out the stars, naming the constellations and sharing their stories. And then they fell into companionable silence, not uncomfortable, not needing small talk.

Serena's heartbeat slowed, her muscles relaxed—she started to feel more at ease in her surroundings.

To appreciate the twinkling of the stars, the beauty of the lake, the placid pine trees waving on the distant shore.

"Serena," he said from behind her.

It felt like the first time he had ever said her name. Maybe it was. But she knew that she would always remember the soft way he said it.

He kissed the downy hair at the nape of her neck, he caught the secret spot where her tender nerves sent shivers throughout her body.

She wanted to turn around, to throw her arms around him and tell him to take her.

Take her now.

It was time, wasn't it?

She had waited all day, all her life, for this moment.

But she knew that he intended to pace them. It would do her no good to rush.

He knew what he wanted, how he wanted it, and he knew how to give her pleasure she was sure.

She trusted him.

And if he wanted her to wait, so be it.

Still, she was wet and aching, while he had done no more than kiss her neck.

"Look at the stars," he commanded, just as she thought she would explode with her longings. "Look at them. Millions and millions of them."

She followed his gaze, distracted from her longings by the sparkling white pinpoints of light, some so densely placed that they were like clouds.

It had been a long time since she had seen stars that didn't have an ego, a wardrobe manager and an upcoming movie release.

"Scientists say we're descended from apes," Dylan said. "But I like to think we are the children of the stars."

"That's very poetic, especially for a bodyguard, but what do you mean?"

"I'll ignore the slight to my profession," he said with mock severity. "But most people think of the stars being there in the sky, unchanging and unmoving."

"You have to admit, stars have been here longer than we have."

"Maybe so, but there's still a lot of action in the life of a celestial body. Stars are born in an explosion of energy, they change and grow and sparkle and then they die. Everything—all the stages of life—like we do."

"It just takes them billions of years longer and they do it while hurtling through space at speeds we can't even imagine, right?"

"That's what I mean. Risks and reversals, terror and triumph. But they do it, just like we do. How big is that country of yours?"

Startled by his sudden change of topic and the vastness of the sky in front of her, she almost couldn't remember what country he was thinking of.

But then, the words and facts came to her, the necessities of a well-informed royal.

She rattled off the square kilometers, converting it to square miles because Americans still didn't use the metric system, and then added the population, gross national product, and import-export ratio since she had used each of these facts in a speech before New York businessmen and Washington politicians.

"Dinky country," he muttered.

"I'll have you know that our country is among the most civilized of Europe! We have the highest literacy rate, the lowest infant mortality rate, the—"

"And none of it matters when you look at all this," he said calmly, pointing to the night sky.

"Don't make your own prison, Princess. Don't close yourself up. And don't imprison your sons."

"I'm not! I'm not the one who wants it like this. I wanted my marriage to work! I wanted to represent my country well and not appear every week on some tabloid cover!" She knew her voice had risen dramatically, nearly hysterically. "I wanted to be a good mother."

"I'm sure you are."

"Nothing turned out the way I thought it would," she said.

She trembled and shook and she was sure, even in darkness, that her skin had crimsoned with emotion.

"So what happened?" he asked blandly.

"It wasn't a fairy-tale romance. It wasn't love at first sight or second sight or any sight at all," she confessed, hearing the words aloud for the first time. All that she had denied for so long. Even to herself. "It wasn't me being swept off my feet or him falling head over heels. It was an arranged marriage between noble families and I was just young enough and just stupid enough to think he loved me."

"You and the rest of the world."

"No, I should have known. All that time, his heart belonged to Lady Jane Howard. I almost feel sorry for him and certainly, I feel sorry for her. She's waited years for him."

"Why'd he marry you? I mean, you're beautiful

and charming and wonderful and all that—but why not Lady Jane if she's the woman he loves?"

"Because I come from the right family, because there was no scandal attached to any of my far-flung relatives and, perhaps most importantly, I was a virgin and a physical examination revealed that I could bear strong, healthy children."

"You actually had a physical to determine...?"

"And a DNA test."

"You're kidding."

"The palace insisted on it."

"And why didn't he marry Lady Jane? Didn't she pass the test?"

"I don't know that she was ever given the opportunity to try. She's from a lesser family, she was divorced, and she was considered too old. But if she had left our family alone, I think my ex-husband could have learned to love me. Maybe."

"You don't 'learn' to love anyone. It either happens or it doesn't."

"Well, we can disagree about that. But it doesn't matter now. Now the battle is over my sons. I want my sons to succeed to the throne without being cast aside simply because their father never loved me and regards me as little more than a breeding cow! I know the price to keep my sons safe from royal intrigue is to disappear, disappear so completely that Lady Jane Howard can take my place."

"Lady Jane Howard could never replace you...."

"Oh, yes, she could. And she will. Prince Franco

wishes to marry her and he will have his way, regardless of what the polls say. We've produced an heir—and a spare—so he feels free to pursue his happiness. She has to take my place as a princess, as a wife, even...even as a mother. And I've come to understand that my country is damaged by the turmoil of our family. It would be better for my country if I disappeared. Better for my sons as well. Maybe even better for me.''

"How can you think like that? How can you sacrifice yourself?''

"You thought like that when you resigned from the Secret Service. You were protecting a president.''

"But I didn't have to give up everything you're giving up.''

"Oh, really?''

"Well, maybe just a little.''

He reached out and caressed her cheek, wiping away a tear she hadn't known she shed. His tenderness was more unbearable than the gruff masculine arrogance that was his stance.

"You don't have to do anything you don't want to. That's the truth here, but it's also truth for you back in your own country. You don't have to go away. You don't have to go into exile.''

"Why do you care?'' she begged, the tears now pouring, tears that she had held back so many, many times in her very public life. "Dylan, we only have tonight. I want just one night of your life and then

I want you to forget me. Why do you care what I do later?"

He stared at her long and hard. She wasn't sure if he was angry but the intensity of his look began to frighten her. She felt a trembling within her, all of her awakened sexuality converted to fear.

"Why do you care?" she repeated.

"Because...because..." He uttered a harsh oath, adding with a cry, "Because I'm an American and we Americans take freedom very seriously!"

He stalked away from her, toward the house. She followed, wishing she could make him understand. She tugged at his sleeve and he whirled around— she thought he was angry, but even in the darkness of night, she could see sorrow, not anger, moved him.

"I'm sorry," he said. "That was selfish of me. I was thinking of how I would feel."

"Are you sure that's how you would feel? What if your children were involved?"

He shook his head, stricken.

"I don't have any and I don't know what I'd do if did."

"Trust me. You and I are alike. You'd make the same choice if it meant your children's future. You sacrificed so much for Charlotte and for your mother and for your president—you'd do even more for your own children."

"I can't save you, can I?"

"No," she said simply. "You're a handsome and

wonderful knight in shining armor, but this is not a battle you can win. But give me tonight. And then forget about me.''

''You're going to be awfully hard to forget.''

''Do your best.''

He swept her up into his arms, kissing her as she had wanted, as she had waited for, as she had dreamed of all her life.

If there were only two kinds of people in the world, cold-blooded cynics and romantic fools, she knew she had been the biggest fool of them all.

Heaven help her, she was a romantic.

Chapter Fifteen

As he carried her into the upstairs bedroom, he didn't tell her that the first time is for passion. The first time is to quell the urgency of appetite so that lovers can slowly consume the hours and the wonders of the second, third and fourth times.

When he lit the kerosene bedside lamp, he didn't tell her that the first time could be awkward, more so for a woman.

He adjusted the light to a warm, forgiving glow.

Although imbued with a private, modest nature, he had never been embarrassed or ashamed of his body. Clothed or naked.

But some women he had made love to had wanted to hide their flesh under cover of darkness or sheets while others had flaunted their hard, taut bodies with a bravado and pride that was wrenching.

Serena was neither of these extremes. She lay back on the worn ivory sheets and stared as he pulled his T-shirt up over his head.

Ordinarily, he would undress a woman first, and

when at last he threw off his own restraining fabrics, he had a naked woman before him to spur his ardor. He had always found the sight of a naked woman beautiful, the female body so mysterious and divine.

This time, however, he wanted to undress himself first. Not so that he could flaunt himself to her, not because he would be unable to control himself if she were unclothed before him. No, he undressed because he wanted Serena to have every opportunity to back out.

It was one thing to drive up from Chicago with carnal intentions—it was another to actually make love to a man she barely knew and whom she had promised never to see again.

And from whom she had extracted the same promise.

He felt an unutterable sadness thinking of how there could be nothing more between them, not even an innocent second date, not even a lingering morning after.

In his youth, the prospect of a beautiful woman in his bed for one night—and only one night— would have thrilled him.

Some of his buddies called such a woman "A Sure Thing."

But he was older now, with feelings young men don't have.

He wanted to say so much, to confess so much about his heart, how much love he had discovered in a single day. He wanted no sure things. He welcomed all the risks and reprisals of morning—but he couldn't.

She was a mother and a princess and was determined to remain both.

Then he shoved aside his regrets and his wishes—this night was not about him, this was for her.

As he undressed, he half expected her to run crying into the bathroom, courage having forsaken her. If that happened, he knew that no matter how excited he was, no matter the racing of his pulse, he would pull his clothes back on and without complaint or comment drive her back to Chicago.

Or simply sit with her in this house, his sanctuary, with his fleshly needs in check.

Whatever she wanted, whatever she needed, whatever she asked for.

He tugged at his belt, at first impatient with the clasp and then he remembered himself. He slowed his hands and paused at each movement, not because he was prideful or because he wanted her lingering admiration, but because he wanted her to know what she was getting.

She was getting a man. A real man, not a puppet prince who was—if rumors were to be believed—at least three inches too short to dance with her and too weak to carry her to a royal bed. At the very least, the prince must be a fool if he couldn't see the treasure that was his wife.

So Serena would have no prince tonight. She was

getting a man with hard, gristled muscles across his chest and shoulders—the kind of muscles that aren't made in a yuppie gym but are forged by the needs of his profession. She was getting a man with an ugly scar on his abdomen from a gunshot wound that had nearly been the death of him. She was getting a man whose fingernails were not buffed, whose hair fell past his ears.

She sat up and he froze, certain she had reconsidered this foolish venture. Instead, she spread her legs, grabbed his jeans waistband and yanked him to her. Hard. He opened his mouth in shock—he was standing between her legs, his hips scant inches from her upturned face.

"Unzip your pants," she said, a feral amusement in her voice at war with the trembling of her rosebud lips.

"I...uh...I..."

"Never, ever disobey the direct command of a princess," she said, wagging her finger at him.

He didn't take orders from a woman. Didn't take orders from anyone, for that matter. But he liked this. He liked a woman playing with her pleasure. He especially admired this woman. He admired her grit.

"Okay," he said. "Okay...Your Royal Highness."

"That's better." She smiled, satisfied.

He unzipped himself, feeling a little like a beefcake stripper. She watched with widened eyes. He pulled down his jeans and then his boxer briefs. He stood before her, naked and hard. Her lips paled and she licked away their dryness. She reached out to touch him, to touch the manhood that glistened and throbbed. He grabbed her wrist.

"Not so fast," he said.

If she touched him now, he knew he might lose control of himself. And he couldn't do that. He intended to maintain his control until she had had her pleasure, until she was spent and certain of the rightness of what she was doing.

He pulled her to her feet and assured of her steadiness, relinquished his grip. Then he sprawled down on the soft bed, like a lion that is sated. And yet, he was not. She stood, confused and yet transfixed by his nakedness.

"Your turn," he said with marked casualness. "Get undressed."

"Wha...?"

He wagged his finger at her.

"Never, ever disobey the direct command of your lover."

EXTRAORDINARY?

That was an understatement.

She was halfway around the world from her country, in a cabin the size of her jewelry storage vault, and at her feet was a naked man who looked like a Greek god.

A Greek god who was hers to command.

And hers to obey.

Oh, sure, he had a deliciously wicked smile on his face, his eyes twinkled knowingly and his body was tensed, ready for action. He had told her—no, commanded her—to undress as if he were a pasha and she his harem slave. And he showed not a trace of doubt that she would disobey him.

Yet, Serena trusted that she could reconsider the temptations, call an abrupt halt to their tryst and he would dress without a grumble and lay not a hand on her.

Armed with this trust, she did his bidding, pulling her T-shirt up over her head to reveal a bra made of featherlight lace and silk. She did so with a surprising treasure of confidence that she would give up nothing this night that she did not want to give. And that he would do only what she willed and then, with discretion, carry the secrets of this night unspoken to his grave.

She dropped a strap across her shoulder. And then another. Serena reveled in his quick intake of breath, the shudder of the muscles that crisscrossed his abdomen.

Teasing him now, she shimmied out of her bra, dropped it on the floor.

With a sudden jolt of her natural modesty, she stood with her arms crossed carefully in front of her.

This was the hard part, she thought. Two pregnancies. Nursing for several months after the birth of each son. No longer a coltish girl of twenty. Her

ex-husband having always regarded her as a necessary duty. It was one thing to be admired by the
crowds at the palace or by the news reporters of a
distant land when she was dressed in designer suits
and gowns and corseted within an inch of her suf-
focation.

This was up close and real.

And time had a funny way of being more forgiving of a man's body.

Her breasts ached to be touched by Dylan, she
wanted his caresses. But paralyzed by her fear of his
disapproval, she stood trembling. Wet to her core,
though he had not even touched her.

"You're beautiful, Princess," he assured her,
leaning up, entwining his fingers in hers, pulling
apart her barrier.

As her breasts came free, she studied his reaction
carefully. Ready to bolt if the humiliation proved
too great. But he showed not a flicker of distaste.
Rather, the dark chocolate centers of his eyes dilated
and she knew he found her...beautiful.

"Come here," he growled.

She was only too happy to obey. She straddled
him and he cupped her breasts in his hands, each of
his calluses rubbing raw her pale, smooth skin. She
reached beneath her, to the triangle of his maleness.

"Whoa, not so fast," he exclaimed again, his
broad hand covering hers. "If you touch me there,
I won't last very long."

"And then it will be over? All over?"

"No, darlin', then I'll just have to take my time the second time around. And the third. And the fourth."

"How many times...?"

"As often as you want. Or until I die. Either way, I'll have a smile on my face," he said.

With an expert hand, he tugged down her jeans and panties. She kicked the clothing from her ankles. She bucked against his hand as he touched the mound of her sex. They both knew she was as ardent and wanting as he was.

"No, no, I don't want it to be like this," he said with a jagged edge to his voice. "I want it to be perfect...perfect for a princess."

"I'm not a princess now," she replied. "Just for tonight, don't treat me like royalty. Treat me like your woman."

He blinked once at her, staring then to find the truth in her eyes. And, with a lightning speed that thrilled as it sent a tremor of fear throughout her, he brought her down beneath his weight. He splayed her hands above her head, entering her sharply and precisely. She cried out once in surprise and then more softly in pleasure as he thrust deep within her.

As he brought her to ecstasy, she forgot where she was, what she was, who she was, but she became sure of only one thing: she wasn't a princess any longer.

She was Dylan's woman.

SERENA SLEPT SOUNDLY, the flat sheet pulled out from its nurses' corners and wrapped around them like a cocoon. Her dreams were sighs of contentment and fulfillment, with the future tucked away, momentarily forgotten.

He lay awake. Thinking. Watching as her thick fringe of lashes fluttered with wakefulness.

"What if I couldn't give you up?" he asked as she stirred in his arms.

"You have to," she murmured, turning to rest her head on his chest. "You have to."

"What if I couldn't?"

Her eyes flew open. "You have to," she said firmly. "Don't scare me."

"I don't mean to scare you. I just think we need to recognize the truth. Something happened when we made love. Didn't you feel it? It was something more than sex."

"Yes, I did feel it," she admitted. "But how we feel doesn't change things."

"It doesn't?"

"No. My sons and my country are relying on me. I can't change anything about tomorrow."

"But what if we could?" Dylan asked. "We're still young. We can make this our second chance. We can marry. We can have a family together. We can start over. We can make the life we want, the life we've dreamed about. We can act selfishly, for once in our lives."

She sat up, touching her finger to his lips. "Don't talk like that. We aren't selfish people."

"We could be!"

"Would you, could you love a woman who would sacrifice her sons or her country for her own selfish gain?"

He shook his head. "No, I guess I couldn't."

"Then we can't be selfish. We just can't. A lot of people could get hurt if we think just of ourselves. We have to play by the rules."

"Damn the rules."

"You didn't mind them before."

"I didn't know the rules were so harsh."

"No, I guess I didn't, either."

She lay down again spoon-wise to him. He pulled her close to him, memorizing the feel of her round buttocks against his stomach, the way her toes just reached his ankles, the scent of talc and rose that lingered in her hair.

"So tell me about the life we could have had," she whispered.

He closed his eyes against the pain. "We'd live in the old neighborhood," he said. "I don't believe in discarding your friends because you have come into money. So we'd have a house with…three bedrooms, a bath on the second floor and a basketball hoop in the driveway."

"What would we do in our house? Start with Sunday. It's my favorite day of the week."

"Mine, too," he said, although he hadn't ever

given it much thought before. "I'd wake you early in the morning, with kisses."

"Kisses. I like that."

"I'd kiss you here. And here. And here. And I'd tell you it was time to get up because we'd have to go to church and..."

"Would I roll over and put my arms around you?"

"Yeah. Yeah, that's exactly what you'd do. Darlin', are those tears?"

"Ignore them."

"I can't."

"You have to. Go back to Sunday. Tell me all about Sunday. Make love to me again as if it were Sunday."

Chapter Sixteen

"Cuthbert, it's me again."

"Where the hell are you now? And where's that princess?"

"Around."

"Is she with a man?"

"You know, Cuthbert, do you think it's any of your business?"

"Of course it's my business. It's my only business. MacPhail, this situation is getting out of hand. The older boy, I mean, His Royal Highness the Prince of Cornith, has called me personally."

"Good for him," Dylan muttered.

"Huh? Well, anyhow, he was complaining because I told him his damn mother—excuse me, Her Royal Highness—is too ill to speak to him. The juvenile delinquent—I mean, His Royal Highness—said he'll issue a royal proclamation on his coronation day firing me from my post and exiling me from the country."

"Like I said—good for him. I don't know him but I have a lot more respect for him now."

"MacPhail, you don't understand the first thing about our country. He can't fire me. This is a hereditary job. Been in my family for four centuries."

Dylan stood in his study, a pine-paneled hideaway converted from a farmhouse attic. He tugged absently at the drawstring of his flannel pajama bottoms and thought of the woman who slept downstairs in his bed wearing the top that matched his bottoms.

"I'll call you in a few hours."

"That's not good enough, MacPhail. After I talked to that…that child…I realized that as Lord of the Chamber I have the right and the duty to deploy the men under my command to locate her and bring her back to His Most Royal Highness Prince Franco."

"You mean her ex-husband. The one who wants to exile her to some Arctic Island."

There was a high-pitched whistling sound.

"How do you know about the Isle of Whit?"

"She told me about it. When I had her. Remember? I had her for a while. She talked."

"I'll bet she did. Wrapped you around her little finger. Am I to understand you sympathize with her?" Cuthbert asked smartly.

Dylan chose his next words carefully, although he would have—in any other situation—told Cuthbert differently.

"I'm doing my job, Cuthbert," he said. "I'll bring her in tomorrow. I'll call you first light."

"I'm not waiting for a phone call. I'm coming after you. Myself."

"I'll call you."

"How do I know you aren't going to find the princess and run off into the sunset with her, like in all those ungodly sentimental American movies?"

"Because I'm more interested in the money," Dylan said flatly.

It was an answer that would have been true yesterday. And because it would have been true yesterday, Cuthbert seemed to accept it.

"All right, MacPhail, you keep thinking about that money. And give me a number where you are," he added. "Give me the number on that cell phone of yours. I'm calling you every two hours. On the hour. Until you get her in."

"I don't give out this number."

Cuthbert issued a loud harrumph. "Are you hiding something from me? Because if you are, I swear..."

"Of course not."

"Then give me the number. And if you don't have Her Royal Highness in here by eight in the morning, I'm coming after her myself. And I'll have a posse consisting of every reporter and gossip hound in the country."

"All right, all right," Dylan said wearily.

He gave Cuthbert his cell phone number, hung up

and spent the next several minutes thinking about Serena's options.

There were only two.

Make a run for it with him.

Or go back begging for mercy.

He walked upstairs to the bedroom. She slept curled against his pillow with a slim, pale arm covering her face. For the first time, he noticed the double picture frame on the nightstand.

He wondered when she had had time to put it there.

Her two sons beamed at him.

The older one was wearing a navy blue sport coat with a crest on its breast pocket and a striped tie on a white shirt. His smile was friendly, but hinted at a strength of personality. He must be the Prince of Cornith—and the one who would one day give Cuthbert his just deserts.

The younger one wore a mud-splattered soccer uniform and a triumphant, toothy grin.

They both looked like her.

He thought of his mother, of all she had done for him and his sister. Of all she had sacrificed and all she had worked for, especially after she was left on her own as a widow. She had done it all because she was a mother. And he and his sister had always respected that, honored that, cherished that. Even when they didn't understand it. And he knew that his mother would never have had it any other way.

Dylan picked up the frame and looked at the two boys again.

Serena had only one option. He could see that now.

He had to cut her loose. And he had to do it in such a way that she wouldn't look back.

DYLAN'S WOMAN awoke sensuously, savoring the musk-and-citrus scent of her man on the pillow which she hugged against her breast. She stretched, felt a delicious ache from her loins to the tips of her toes, a last remnant of their ardent lovemaking.

So this was what all the excitement was about!

Making love was deserving of every sonnet, every song, every movie, every book and every play. It was worth every heartbreak, every marriage vow, every sigh and every sacrifice. Making love to the man she loved was worth everything.

And she knew she loved him. Knew it the first time as he entered her. Knew that she couldn't surrender her self-control nor her body to any man but Dylan. And knew in that moment of ecstatic relinquishment of control that the grudging admiration or the amusement or the delight she had felt for him were just pieces that fit together into the whole tapestry of her love for him.

And she knew to the core of her being that he felt the same way for her. For he had shown her three, four...or was it five?...times until, as dawn approached, she had pleaded for sleep.

They had packed a lifetime of memories into a single night.

She glanced at the alarm clock on the nightstand. Seven-thirty. She had had perhaps two hours rest, but she knew she wouldn't go back to sleep. But as her eyes focused on the tiny double frame that she took with her to every corner of the earth, a dark thought came to her.

It was terribly messy and unwise to fall in love, as Lady Bostwick pointed out every afternoon while watching her soap operas. Serena had never paid much attention to the television shows, but she wondered now if she had missed some kernels of wisdom on how to deal with the messiness and foolishness of falling in love.

Especially waking up in love the morning after a one-night stand.

The prospect of her sons' future hung heavily over her, marring the bliss. Their faces, with innocent and unknowing happiness, beamed at her.

She knew what she had to do but it was no less painful for knowing it.

She had to have the strength to walk away.

Even if he begged her to stay.

"Your turn, Princess," Dylan said, emerging from the bathroom wearing jeans and a T-shirt. He combed his wet hair back from his forehead but a mischievous lock fell back onto his face. "Get up. It's your turn in the bathroom. I put out a clean towel, but I'm afraid the accommodations are primitive compared to what you're used to."

She sat up in bed, her blood turning to ice. "Wha...what did you say?"

But it wasn't what he said so much as how he said it. The nonchalant arrogance in his voice. The carefree way he sauntered around the room.

He glanced at her and then returned to combing his hair in front of the full-length mirror hung behind the bedroom door.

"I said it was your turn to use the bathroom. I showered first because I figured you could use a few extra minutes of sleep. But we've got to be on the road in less than twenty. I promised Cuthbert that we'd be back. By the way, last night..." He turned around, flashing her a charming smile that carried no warmth. "Last night was great, Princess."

He said more as he combed his hair and dressed. Much more. How it was fun. How she was really good in bed. How last night would be a wonderful memory. It was a night he would never forget. Did she have fun, too?

He also said she had twenty minutes to get dressed. He didn't know how long Cuthbert could be placated. He thought they'd stop at the drive-through fast-food place for a doughnut along the way. To save time. By the way, did she like doughnuts?

Serena stared at him blankly. And then, with growing horror, understood the terrible truth.

The unwise truth. The messy truth.

She had fallen in love with a man who felt nothing for her. Absolutely nothing. Other than, as he put it while he drew back the sheets and gave her a lazy once-over, she had a "fantastic bod."

When he had told her he couldn't let her go, when he begged her to renounce everything for him, had he been lying? Worse, was it only a dream?

As he trotted downstairs, she felt paralyzed—stunned and betrayed. Naked in a soiled way, unlike all the hours they had reverently explored each other's bodies.

She wanted to yank back the sheets to cover herself and let the tears come.

But she had been humiliated before. Publicly and privately. Her ex-husband and the scheming, manipulative lords and ladies of the court were experts at torturing a soul without laying a hand on the body.

She knew how to put on a brave face. How to smile when she felt like crying. How to act as if she had not a care in the world when she felt crushed and low.

"You have a great bod, too," she said to the empty room, tilting her chin up high. She walked to the bathroom with all the dignity of the first ship of a military regatta. She brushed away a tear from her cheek. "It was a great night. Lots of fun, lots of laughs. I'll never forget you, either."

As she closed the door behind her, she caught a glimpse of herself in the mirror. Her hair was snipped short, sun-kissed and tousled. Her eyes rimmed red with captive grief. Her mouth swollen from a thousand kisses. She sniffed her wrist. Dylan. She had his scent on her. She wondered if she'd ever get rid of it.

As she must.

She had her sons to think of.

Maybe Dylan's casual attitude about their night together was a blessing in disguise. Because now she didn't have to face the horrific possibility of shortchanging her sons.

If he had begged her to stay, she wasn't sure she'd have the strength to leave him.

Now she knew exactly what she was doing, when for the past twenty-four hours she had felt adrift without the predictability of her station.

She wondered vaguely what he thought of her—if he thought she slept with many men, as the magazines and tabloids claimed.

The previous year there had been no less than a dozen men who cashed in on stories of being the love of her life—one of them was a cavalry officer billeted just a half mile from the castle and that fact alone made plausible the man's lie.

Did Dylan think of their night together as satisfying in a strictly athletic sort of way?

Would he—and this thought terrified her—be such a cad as to brag to his buddies about his triumph?

Worse, would he sell his story?

She couldn't accuse him of having taken advantage of her, of having not played by the rules. Rules she had laid down.

He was a man who liked his pleasures and gave as good as he got. And he was simply acknowledging what was true, what was real, what had been agreed upon.

It was a one-night stand. A lot of fun, a pleasure, a memory. But just that and nothing more.

She rued her naivete. She had always been a woman to face facts squarely and she would recover. Would survive. Would even thrive again. Someday. She would mourn in private when no one could see her pain.

She turned the water on, scalding and then punishingly cold. She washed every inch of herself with grief and self-reproach. She knew she had to blur every memory of him or else she could not bear to leave him, to face the long days alone, to survive and sacrifice for her sons and her country.

How could she wash away the love she felt for him?

A fool, she told herself many times as she scrubbed until her skin was crimson. You have been a fool.

When she ventured out of the bathroom, she found he was mercifully gone. She dressed quickly, refusing to look directly at the bed. Jeans, her T-shirt and sneakers. She remembered that her windbreaker was downstairs in the living room armoire.

She ran downstairs, drawn to the kitchen's strong coffee smell. Just before she walked through the door, she pinched her cheeks and took three quick breaths.

She was a princess and she was determined to act like one.

A wasted effort. He wasn't in the kitchen, but was nursing his coffee on the back porch. An opened newspaper and his cell phone were on the wrought iron table next to him.

She poured herself a cup, grateful for its too strong taste and stepped out into the damp, summer morning.

"It's been twenty minutes," she said, summoning a breezy royal command. "Please prepare the car, if you will."

He looked up sharply. Their eyes met, she saw the boyish blue of his eyes shimmer with tears, and then he looked away.

Closing his eyes and pressing his lips together as if he were stopping himself from exploding.

"Sunday," he whispered. "It's Sunday."

"No, it's not," she corrected. "It's Thursday morning and...oh, Dylan. Sunday."

"Yes."

"Our favorite day of the week. An ordinary day. But our favorite."

Her heart soared, even as she felt the enormity of his pain. And the enormity of their sorrow.

She knew him, with a lover's certainty.

"You love me," she said softly. "You love me as much as I love you."

He sighed, shaking his head as if he could rewrite the truth with his denial.

"Yes," he said. "I love you and I know I have to let you go. But don't you see? I have to make you leave. For your own good. For your sons—I know all of that. But I can't seem to do a very good job of it. Because I can't tell you that it's just been fun or it's just been a memory—I have to tell you that I love you. But I have to tell you to go...and don't look back."

She closed her eyes against the contradiction of joy and sorrow. She heard the scrape of the chair legs as he stood up. He took her into his arms and she buried her head into his chest.

"I love you," he repeated. "I didn't mean to fall in love with you, but I did. Sometime last night it happened. Like a thief in my heart."

She lifted her head. He brushed away the damp wisps of her hair.

"I love you, too," she confessed.

Then he kissed her long and hard.

The phone rang.

He reached out to the table. But the cell phone was silent.

He looked at the door to the kitchen and muttered a tight, foul oath.

"Dylan, what's the matter?"

"No one knows my phone number."

"Then who could be calling?"

"Serena, I've failed you. My love, I have failed you," he said, stricken.

He strode to the kitchen, yanking the house phone from the wall.

He spoke for several seconds into the receiver and then fell silent.

"What is it? What is it?" she begged, coming up behind him.

He looked at her darkly, his breath coming in ragged gulps. He turned away from her, slamming his fist against the wall with a primitive cry.

She winced as she saw the blood spring up on his knuckles.

"Give me that," she said, prying the phone from his other hand.

"Hello?"

"Gotcha," Cuthbert said with malicious pleasure.

Chapter Seventeen

The terms Cuthbert laid out for her were clear and unequivocal. The car was waiting for her at the edge of the cornfield in front of Dylan's house. She was to get into the back seat and be driven back to the Drake Hotel without any stops along the way. She would speak to no one and make no attempt to escape.

She would be dealt with.

"I've already contacted the prince," Cuthbert said. "He is taking a flight from the capital. He should be here early this evening. We'll have time to chat before he arrives."

She didn't have to ask what was at stake.

Her sons.

Her country.

"We have pictures," he warned. "In case you're thinking of denying anything."

"How did you know...?"

Cuthbert laughed without a trace of humor.

"Princess, that's why we hired him."

She glanced at Dylan, leaning against the wall. He was apparently unaware of the blood crisscrossing his knuckles.

"You hired him…?"

"We hired him because we knew you couldn't resist him. It was a trap. And you walked right into it. Look at him closely. See anything familiar about him?"

"I know what he looks like."

"Do you remember a year ago? The scandal at the White House? The Secret Service agent sleeping with the aide to the Speaker of the House? How the information she obtained about the president was so damaging?"

"I already knew that. He told me about it. He told me everything."

"And you still slept with him? Ha! Then you're more of a damn fool than I thought you were. We hired him for a specific purpose and he fulfilled that purpose. He really is quite handsome and sexy in a primitive kind of way, don't you think? Quite irresistible to a woman like you. We made a good hire, don't you think? It was my idea all along. I watched you carefully, watched for your only weakness. You wanted to be loved."

"Oh, my God!" she cried, horrified. "Did he know he was being hired to…?"

"I would be very surprised if he did not."

She looked at Dylan, but he would not meet her eyes.

"I failed you," he whispered. "I failed you. Forgive me, but I failed you."

"Now be a good girl and hand him the phone," Cuthbert said. "I owe him his paycheck—with a little bonus for having done a good job. Not a bad deal to be paid for seducing a princess, wouldn't you say?"

"How much will he be paid?"

Cuthbert named an exorbitant sum. "And that's nothing compared to the price you will pay," he added. "And that your sons will pay."

She was stunned, reeling, the kitchen seeming to spin on an axis.

But she managed to pull herself together and without another word, Serena handed the phone to Dylan and stumbled out the front door of the farmhouse. A black limousine was parked in a ditch beside the cornfield.

From a distance she saw a farmer fixing a tire on a tractor. The sun was already blistering. It was going to be a miserably hot day and it was still May.

On the Isle of Whit there would be snow on the ground. The first crocuses would be poking their heads through the whiteness.

"Good morning, Your Royal Highness."

The driver snapped a crisp salute and opened the door of the car.

She was grateful for one mercy—that she would be alone on the drive to Chicago.

"HOW DID YOU find this number? It's unlisted. Nobody knows it."

"We started tracking you the minute you handed me the phone number on your cell phone. We precisioned the location using equipment so sophisticated that even your CIA is interested in buying it from our defense department. And then we moved in on your house. You've been surrounded by our people for the last two hours."

"How'd you get past...?"

"Your security perimeter wires? We've had navy SEAL-trained men on that one. Nice job, by the way. The wires were quite a trick."

"What the hell did you say to her?"

"I told her to come to her senses," Cuthbert said, not bothering to conceal his triumph. "I told her to think of her duty. And that's one thing Serena knows all about—duty."

"What did you tell her about me?"

"I told her how much we're paying you."

"I don't want the money now."

"And that we hired you for a good reason," Cuthbert said, ignoring the interruption. "Because you're the best. You're the best at so many different things. Marksmanship, crowd control, perimeter sectioning, strategy, fencing, seduction..."

But Dylan didn't even wait for the last string of snide compliments. He vaulted over the kitchen table and flew out the door, screaming her name. He caught up to the limousine just as it backed out of the ditch. He pounded on the jet-black back window.

Screaming her name.

The window glided down.

"Serena, we've got to talk about this!"

"There's nothing to talk about," she said, slipping on oversize black sunglasses. "It's like you said earlier this morning. A lot of fun. Some memories."

"I didn't know when I was hired…"

"Did you sleep with the Speaker's aide?"

"Yes."

"And did she end up with damaging information about the president?"

"Yes, I told you that. God knows I've regretted it to this very day. I was dumb. I was starstruck. I couldn't get over the fact that here I was, working-class stiff from Chicago being courted by a Washington insider. I thought she loved me."

"Maybe you're still a little too starstruck."

"No, Princess, that's not it…."

"It doesn't matter, Dylan, and maybe it's better that I think of you as being a tad mercenary. After all, I have the rest of my life and my sons' lives to consider. Don't embarrass me further, Dylan, and don't put my children's future in jeopardy."

"But…"

"If any part of you is a gentleman, you will do as I ask and never attempt to contact me again. I beg that of you."

That stopped him dead in his tracks.

He held his hands up in surrender to her will and backed off three steps.

"Driver," she said. "The window."

The glass glided shut and the car shuddered out of the ditch and disappeared into a curtain of early cornstalks and a billowing cloud of rich Wisconsin soil.

"I'M NOT DRESSING UP in a maid's costume," Charlotte said, shaking her head implacably. "I don't do maid."

"I'm not asking you to actually be a maid," Dylan corrected. "I'm just asking you to get me in there. I'll take care of the rest."

"I don't care. I'm not being a maid."

She put her coffee mug down on the dining room table and absently wiped at the powdered sugar left on her plate by her half-eaten doughnut.

"But all you have to do is say, 'Housekeeping' and maybe throw in a, 'New towels, sir?' or, 'Do you want your bed turned down, sir?'"

"Nothing doin'. I look like a cop. I walk like a cop. I talk like a cop. Even if you put me in a dress with a white apron and a funky cap, my appearance is still going to scream, 'Cop!'"

"You've done undercover."

"You're right. I can do drug dealer, murderer, armed robber and extortionist—all of them not very well. But I know I can't do maid at all. I'm just not deferential enough.''

''That's for sure,'' Dylan conceded with a groan. ''But I've got to get into Cuthbert's room.''

''You're not even going to try to see her? A final goodbye? A we'll-always-have-memories hug? A kiss to tide you over until the next life?''

''No. Hopefully she won't even know I've been there at all.''

''You're going to a lot of trouble just to punch out Cuthbert.''

''It's not punching him I want.''

''Then what is it?''

''None of your business.''

She stuck out her tongue at him.

''Well, you've got a good enough reputation around the force that I can pull all kinds of favors,'' she concluded. ''The Chicago police will give you the support you need. But no maid. I'm not going to be a maid. And I can't imagine any of the other guys in my precinct who would volunteer to be a maid.''

''And just how am I going to get to Cuthbert's room?'' Dylan challenged.

The siblings glanced up as the floorboard on the steps creaked. The pink dress. The starched crisp apron. The hair net. The bobby pins holding the ruffled white cardboard hat in place. The sensible rubber-soled shoes. The quiet, sly smile.

''Turndown service, sir?''

"Ma?"

"I'll be a maid if that'll help my children," Mrs. MacPhail said.

Dylan shook his head. "No, way, Ma, this isn't going to work."

"Dylan, I've always wanted to do undercover work. Why should Charlotte have all the fun?"

"You're not doing it, Ma."

"I want you to have your chance to take a swing at this Cuthbert character," Mrs. MacPhail said. "He used you, Dylan. And nobody does that to my boy. Or my girl, either."

"Ma, I don't want to take a swing..."

"Well, I do," Mrs. MacPhail said.

"Brother, you're going about this all wrong," Charlotte argued. "You're so in love with Serena you're not thinking like a professional. You're thinking like an amateur."

"And just how does a pro think, little sister?"

"A pro thinks about weaknesses and how to exploit them."

"Cuthbert's weaknesses? Peppermints and spit-polished shoes."

"Well, I suppose it's a start."

CUTHBERT STARED disdainfully at the five police officers standing in the hallway. Five dress blues. Five matching crew cuts with navy-brimmed caps and leather jackets with the Chicago flag shoulder patch. Five dark aviator frames. One officer was a little taller than the rest and he looked oddly familiar. But when he noticed Cuthbert scrutinizing him, he looked away sharply. Cuthbert concluded that he didn't know the cop—after all, Cuthbert had never willingly met any person who didn't boast at least one hereditary title.

"Let me guess." Cuthbert smirked. "You each want Her Royal Highness's autograph for your mother?"

"No, not at all, Lord Cuthbert," Officer Kerner said, tipping his hat. "We're representatives of the Policeman's Union."

"Oh. You want a donation."

"Not at all, Lord Cuthbert. We…we've admired your work."

"Really?"

"And we feel as fellow officers that your work has been greatly underappreciated. Especially by the media."

"Really?"

"It must be hell traipsing after that princess. And I hope you'll pardon me for saying this, but I don't believe the media hype that she's such a goody two-shoes."

"Yeah," chimed in Officer Kerner's partner. "She seems like a real—"

"She is," Cuthbert said blandly.

"We brought you…this."

Cuthbert felt his fingers quiver as he stared at the proffered box.

"Consider it a professional courtesy," Officer Kerner said.

"A token of our admiration," his partner added.

"May we come in for a quick visit?" Kerner said. "We don't want to impose on your time...."

"No, no, come in."

"We know you're a busy man, but we'd be so interested in hearing about your experiences...."

Cuthbert smiled lazily. "I think I have a few moments for a chat."

Sitting on the couch, greedily enjoying the first bite of the candies the officers had brought him, he hardly noticed how only four of them sat down.

Chapter Eighteen

"His Royal Highness, the Crown Prince Franco."

She had dreaded this confrontation from the moment six hours before when Cuthbert had, with barely concealed glee, told her that her ex-husband was flying out from the capital.

Mustering her dignity, Serena curtsied as low as protocol demanded. She heard the swipe of the Prince's heels on the plush carpet of the hotel room, felt rather than saw the cursory bow he gave her.

She looked up to see her two sons enter the room just as Cuthbert launched into the list of their many hereditary titles. Never good at ceremonial greetings, her sons enveloped her in a double bear hug.

"Oh, I'm so glad to see you!" she exclaimed. "I've missed you."

"We've missed you," Erik conceded bashfully.

"Yeah, Mom, it's good to see you," Vlad said.

But her spontaneous joy was quickly replaced with a horrified realization. Erik and Vlad were to be witness to her humiliation, to her shame and to the unraveling of their confident futures.

Cuthbert coughed. "And Her Ladyship Jane Howard of Glaxon-Hapsburg," he said.

Serena struggled to maintain her dignity as the older woman entered the room, dressed in a pink bouclé Chanel suit with beige-and-black spectator pumps. Her auburn hair was perfectly coifed in a French twist.

Serena ruefully looked down at her own jeans and sneakers. Maybe she had never truly been meant for royalty.

"Your Highness," Lady Jane murmured, as she curtsied to Serena. Then she stood beside Franco, glancing up at him with a look that communicated love and support.

In that moment, seeing the two lovers together, Serena knew that she had never had a chance. Never had a chance to win the love of her husband. He could never have learned to love Serena. His heart had always belonged to Lady Jane Howard. How much happier they all would have been if Franco could have married the one woman he had loved!

Although facing certain exile and horrific consequences for her indiscretion, Serena found she could not begrudge the couple their long-awaited happiness together.

"If you don't mind my inquiring, what's happened to your hair?" Franco asked.

"I cut it," Serena admitted, surprised that he had noticed.

"Cool," Erik said.

"It's quite becoming," Lady Jane said.

"All right, boys, Serena, let's sit down," Prince Franco said briskly, taking a chair by the couch. "Lord Cuthbert, let's get this over with. You said it was urgent."

Serena steadied herself enough to sit down on the couch. Erik took the upholstered chair on the other side of the coffee table. Vlad sat beside his mother. Lady Jane discreetly moved to an armchair by the window. Prince Franco cleared his throat.

"Do the boys have to be here for this?" Serena asked.

"Yes," Erik said firmly. "And we are not boys any longer, Mother."

"This won't take long, Your Highness," Cuthbert said, laying a manila envelope on the coffee table. "Your Highness, Sire, we have pictures of the princess in the arms of a certain Dylan MacPhail, taken just this morning. He is the former secret service agent recently dismissed..."

"Resigned," Serena said.

Cuthbert shot her a pitying glance.

"Resigned, dismissed, disgraced, whatever." He looked at Franco. "We discussed him last week."

Serena's heart sank. Dylan had been hired with her ex-husband's knowledge. It must have been just as Cuthbert said—that it was his skills at seduction which were most highly prized. She had been such a fool, such a fool.

"You hired him to provide what specific security service?" Franco asked, elegantly thin fingers poised above the envelope.

"None, Your Highness," Cuthbert said smugly. "We knew that women have always found Dylan MacPhail irresistible."

"MacPhail," Lady Jane pondered. "Isn't he the Secret Service agent from whom the lovely aide to the Speaker of the House was able to elicit certain embarrassing information regarding presidential fund-raising?"

"You're so right, Lady Jane!" Cuthbert said. "He has a certain brutish quality that women find attractive—and he possesses strong appetites that leave him vulnerable to being used. The Speaker's aide photographed files in his home while he slept like a sated lion."

"So why should we hire such a man?" Franco asked.

"In the past, the princess has been too crafty at setting up her trysts for us to get proof of her infidelities to the throne."

"I was never unfaithful!" Serena cried out.

"Did you or did you not make love to Dylan MacPhail?" Cuthbert demanded.

She looked first at her elder son and then at her younger. At her ex-husband and at Lady Jane, who had turned away to look out upon the busy Chicago streets. There would be no mercy, Serena thought dismally.

"Yes...yes, I did make love to him," she confessed.

"Well, I've certainly heard enough," Erik said, clasping his hands together. "Lord Cuthbert, I'm not waiting for my coronation. You're fired."

"No, Erik, don't be foolish!" Serena cried out. She quickly shot a glance at her ex-husband to see if he was angered by their son's protectiveness toward her. But Franco's expression was unreadable.

"You can't fire me, Erik." Cuthbert sneered at the young prince. "I am the Lord of the Chamber. A hereditary title. My family has held this position for over four hundred—"

"Fired," Prince Franco interrupted.

Serena sat bolt upright.

"I have done my duty by the crown!" Cuthbert protested, his face beet red. "I have given you the opportunity to strike these two sons and this princess from the succession. Or at the very least rehabilitate your image. You can remarry without any entanglements from the past."

"But I want the entanglements of the past," Franco said. "They are my family. And, although I was never able to make Serena happy and she was never the love of my life, I will always cherish her because she is the mother of my sons."

"And that is how it should be," Lady Jane said, rising from her chair. "If you will pardon me for speaking plainly, Your Highness, you are the mother of the princes and you hold a special place in the realm into which I can never insert myself. And a special place in your sons' lives that I cannot and should not interfere with. Even should the prince do me the great honor of marrying me."

"Of course I'm going to marry you!" Franco exclaimed.

Serena stared into the eyes of her rival and found...warmth and friendship.

"Thank you, Lady Jane," she said.

"And you, Lord Cuthbert, you heard my son. You're fired," Franco repeated. "I have listened to you for too long. As Lady Jane has pointed out to me on numerous occasions, I have been lucky enough to find my happiness and Serena should be let alone to find her happiness."

Cuthbert sputtered grievously. Serena looked at her ex-husband and mouthed a thank-you.

"No, no," Franco said. "I owe you an apology, Serena. We may have married because of duty but there is no reason that you should suffer any longer because of it."

"But, but, Your Highness, look at these pictures!" Cuthbert cried out.

He flipped open the folder, revealing...nothing.

"Where are those damn pictures?" Cuthbert demanded loudly. "We had pictures of her in his arms—on the deck of his house. He wasn't even wearing a shirt. Where are the negatives?"

"Yes, I should say," said Franco, rising. "Where are those pictures? And the negatives?"

"What was in the pictures?" Lady Jane asked.

"She was in an embrace..."

"Oh, dear," Serena moaned. "Where are they, Cuthbert?"

"I had them," Cuthbert exclaimed, reaching in his pocket for a comforting peppermint. "They were in my hand just a half hour ago."

"Those pictures could be devastating," Serena said grimly. "If they are ever printed..."

"I'll order an investigation immediately," Cuthbert stated.

"Oh, no, you won't," Erik snapped. "You'll pack your bags and go home."

"Serena, I hope you haven't got your heart set on moving to the Isle of Whit," Prince Franco said.

Serena grinned. "Oh, no, Your Highness, I guess I could be persuaded not to go."

"Why'd you want to go there anyhow?" Vlad asked.

Serena shot a glance at her ex-husband. "Long story," she said. "But it doesn't matter now."

Cuthbert gave a pleading whimper to Prince Franco, who shook his head. Cuthbert looked about the room, searching for an ally. Finding none.

"Very well, Your Highness," he sniffed defeatedly. He bowed stiffly and backed out of the room.

"This is still a disaster," Serena said ruefully, as the door closed behind Cuthbert.

"Oh, Mom, it's all right," Vlad consoled.

"No, it's not. I regret to say that I was indiscreet. Those pictures in the wrong hands could be used to make a public spectacle."

"We'll deal with it when it happens," Prince Franco offered, rising to put a steadying hand on Serena's shoulder. "Worse scandals have overtaken many a royal family."

She looked up at him just as he slipped his other arm around Lady Jane.

"I've found my happiness in being with Jane," he said. "I hope you find yours however you wish it to be. Do you love this MacPhail or was he just a...fling?"

She could not bear to answer that question.

Suddenly, they heard a loud scream from the hallway. The door flung open and Cuthbert, his hands covering his nose, sprawled onto the floor. Blood spurted from between his fingers. After screaming, "Yuck!" Erik said he'd grab some towels from the bathroom.

"Cuthbert, really!" Franco protested. "What has gotten into you?"

"The maid! The maid!" Cuthbert howled. "I have no idea why, but some maid just asked me if I wanted turndown service and when I said I did, she punched me. Punched me right in the nose! And then said something about not messing with her boy."

"These Americans have the oddest customs," Lady Jane Howard observed dryly.

OVER A DINNER brought up to the suite by room service, Serena, Lady Jane, and Prince Franco listened to Erik outline his plans for the future.

"If we're going to bring the country into the twenty-first century, we must modernize our ways of doing business," the young man said, squirting ketchup on his burger. "We must have open markets, a redesigned tariff and taxation system and a partnership with western corporations. I want to study business so that I can do more for our people."

"And you want to be our country's ruler when you are older?" Serena asked.

"Of course, Mother. I am lucky enough that I am born with the responsibility to do what it is I truly want to do."

"I'll hire a tutor to train you in business," Franco suggested. "I know just the gentleman. He's a retired CEO of an international cartel of diamond brokers based in the Netherlands."

"No, father, I want to go to an American university," Erik said quietly. "American businesses are the examples we should be emulating and American businessmen are trained in their own country. There are two universities right here in Chicago."

"I have heard of the university of Chicago," Serena suggested. "They've produced their share of Nobel prize winners in economics."

"But, Mom, Northwestern has a better football team," Erik said.

"All right, you can go to the university," Franco said cautiously. "I suppose I should count my blessings that you want to take the throne at all when so many of my cousins are finding their sons interested in becoming mere playboys."

He glanced at Vlad. "What about you, young man?"

The young man in question looked up guiltily from his plate.

"I don't want to be a prince exactly. I want to be a game master."

"A what?" His parents cried out in unison.

"A game master," Vlad said. "It's somebody who creates and programs computer games."

"Let me guess," Franco said. "We don't teach that at our country's university?"

"No, we don't, sir."

Franco sighed heavily and pushed away his plate.

"Then I shall have to appoint a representative of the throne to maintain guard over you two while you study in America."

"Oh, no, not Cuthbert!" Vlad cried out.

"No," Franco said. "I was thinking of someone much nicer. Your mother, perhaps."

He reached across the table and took Serena's

hand. His smile highlighted the tired lines at the corners of his gray eyes.

"Would you mind being a representative of the throne here in the United States?" he asked. "It would mean you'd have to suffer living with them for four years."

"It would be my pleasure, Your Highness," Serena replied.

"However, there is one problem," Lady Jane said archly, tapping her shell pink fingernails on the table.

"What is that, my love?" Franco asked.

"She will need security."

AFTER DINNER, Erik and Vlad took off their suit jackets and dropped their ties—where else?—on the carpet. Nearly men, yet truly boys, Serena thought. They squirmed excitedly and high-fived each other as they negotiated a victory on a video game hooked up to the hotel's television set.

Lady Jane settled into the couch's plush cushions, reading a paperback with a cup of tea while Franco made phone calls.

Serena paced restlessly. She didn't want to interrupt her sons' fun. She wasn't ready yet to allow her press secretary to announce that she was recovered from the flu. And although she sensed that she and Lady Jane would become friends, she wasn't ready to begin that process with her yet.

She picked up her sons' discarded jackets and

ties, put a few dirty plates on the room service tray and watched the flickering images on the screen.

"Mom, just get out of here," Erik said. "You want to go to him. So go."

"Yeah, go to him," Vlad agreed.

"What? What are you talking about?"

"Him. This guy. MacPhail. You want to see him. So just go already."

"Yeah," Erik said. "We're just going to play for another half hour and then HBO is showing the newest Jean-Claude Van Damme film."

"Yuck," Serena said.

"We knew you'd feel that way," Erik said. "But the international film distribution is so slow most of our citizens won't even get a chance to see this movie."

"Tragic," Serena said.

"When I'm ruler," Erik continued, little noticing his mother's sarcasm, "when I'm ruler, I will ensure that every countryman and woman is given free access to all the Van Damme movies they want."

Serena did a double take.

"Mom, that's why I'm not ready to run a country yet," Erik said with a goofy grin.

"And you're just about to lose the Imperial Star Commander Fleet!" Vlad shrieked.

Franco appeared at the doorway, wearing a dark suit and tie.

"Would you be willing to take a brief trip with

me, Serena?'' He asked. ''Lady Jane has suggested that we interview a security expert immediately.''

Lady Jane peered over her reading glasses.

''Yes, I would be happy to go with you,'' Serena said, knowing what she wanted to do, what she needed to do. ''That's a wonderful idea, Lady Jane.''

Chapter Nineteen

The Wrigleyville neighborhood was quiet. Mothers stood on front porches and leaned out of kitchen windows to call their children in for bedtime. The men sitting on the front stoops said their goodnights. The orange sodium streetlights flickered on along the street. A light drizzle began to fall.

Dylan nursed a solitary beer on the creaking porch swing. He rubbed his newly shorn hair. A regulation one-and-a-half-inch crew cut. He smiled.

Cuthbert had given him a double take, finding him oddly familiar.

But never making the connection. Because Cuthbert hadn't trained into his role as a security expert. He thought breeding was enough.

It wasn't.

His hair felt crisp, his head lighter. Maybe he was getting too old for letting his hair grow out. In the end, he felt more comfortable with his hair short.

Still, that didn't mean he was going to pull his gray suits out of the back of the closet—it just meant that he wasn't looking to be a rebel, looking to reject everything, looking for the bitter feelings.

He took a pull on his beer.

He was thankful his mother was out playing bridge with her girlfriends and that he had given her some bills to cover taking the gang out for dessert and coffee afterward.

She had returned from her afternoon aerobics class with an oddly smug expression. And bruised and scraped fingers. Said she'd hurt them in class, but Dylan couldn't think of any exercise that required cracked knuckles. And she wasn't sweating.

Still, the mystery of his mother's minor injuries and lack of perspiration didn't consume him.

He figured he had a couple of hours left to think about Serena, to linger in his thoughts, to remember every moment and then do what had to be done.

He didn't intend to waste a moment.

Tomorrow he'd have to begin the work of rebuilding his life. He had promised her he'd forget her—and he figured it would take every moment of every day of his life to do what he had promised.

Tucking the negatives back in the envelope, he contemplated the five photographs one more time. They were innocent enough. All against the backdrop of a wooden porch out back of a Victorian farmhouse. A vase of wildflowers on the picnic table. A man in blue jeans, his long hair slicked back wet from a shower. A cup of steaming coffee balanced on the railing. A beautiful woman with a pixielike cap of golden hair and wide doelike eyes.

She photographed well. But then, she always had.

This one—coming into his arms.

That one—she's turning away from him.

The third one—she's kissing him.

The fourth one—they press against each other.

The fifth one—her face turned back toward the house.

That last must have been taken when the phone rang.

Innocent stuff. Innocent enough unless you were a princess with a Cuthbert to contend with.

He knew he shouldn't want to look at them. He should be revolted. And he was. He should be furious at the invasion of his privacy. He should feel betrayed that he had been handpicked to betray her. He should feel like a failure, knowing that if he hadn't been so crazy in love he might have known they were closing in.

And he was all these things.

He should be worrying about his career.

But he wasn't.

His private mission had been successful, turning out to be surprisingly easy as soon as he had done as Charlotte suggested: think about his adversary's weakness.

In this case, love of strong mints, spit-polished shoes and a big ego.

As the officers who had helped him high-fived in

the Drake subbasement, Dylan had quietly considered what to do with the photographs.

His first thought had been that he would go after her, make her listen to him, give these back to her with the negatives, and take a knuckle-breaking swipe at whoever authorized this travesty.

Cuthbert first. Then the Franco character.

But he wouldn't. Slipping out of the Drake with the other men in dress blues, he had concluded that he could only bring her trouble by doing anything more.

He was the kind of trouble that could destroy her and her sons. And he was too much of a man to come between a mother and her children. Even if his heart would always have an emptiness that he hadn't even known existed until she tore it open.

He should destroy these photographs and their negatives. And he would.

He would make himself do it.

Because he knew that keeping these was a risk to her—even if he protected them with his very life. There was always a possibility that he would fail her. And so, as a measure of his love for her, he would burn them.

He still had the baseball she had caught, it was sitting on the windowsill of his bedroom and, knowing his mother, it would stay there for a decade without being disturbed.

He would let Serena think the worst of him. Let her think he betrayed her. Because that might be the only way she would make it through the long days ahead. Because unless she thought he was a bastard, she would be sliced up in two because of her love for him and her allegiance to her children.

She was like him—loyal and true.

He remembered the oath he had taken, with a kiss to the sweet flesh of her palm. He was her knight as surely as if he were from her own country. And he would be so until his dying day, though he would never see her again and she would never know.

"Love you, Princess," he said to no one but himself.

He regarded his beer thoughtfully, decided he wanted no more, and stood up. He had already stacked the wood in the fireplace and lit the match, though it was a warm late spring evening.

But fire was the only way of being absolutely sure nothing was left.

Twenty minutes—the fire should be hot and merciless by now.

A black limousine swooped around the corner. He shoved the photos back in the manila envelope. He reached for his shoulder holster, hanging over the arm of the wicker chair across the table.

The sleek car stopped at the curb.

The passenger door opened before the driver could come around. A thin, stiff-necked man wearing a formal suit stepped out of the limousine and blinked up at the MacPhail residence.

"You look shorter in person," Dylan said, his eyes narrowing with distaste.

"Everyone does," the prince said amiably. "Shorter and thinner in person. Camera adds ten pounds and a few inches up top."

The prince sauntered up the brick-bordered path to the bottom step of the porch.

"Pity I can't figure out a way for the camera to make me look like I have more hair," he said. He smiled and held out his hand. "I should introduce myself. I'm Prince Franco. And you must be Dylan MacPhail."

It was tough for Dylan to refuse to shake hands. It just wasn't in his nature to snub a man or to deny anyone the basic courtesies of greeting.

But then Dylan thought about who he was dealing with. He remembered Serena's description of the Isle of Whit. Of all she was giving up. And the two boys she was doing it for. Of the country she thought she was serving by her exile.

"I oughta take a swing at you," he said. "A good hard swing."

"They warned me that you were an honorable but somewhat primitive man," Franco replied, dropping his hand. "I hope you won't take a punch at me because I wouldn't have the slightest clue how to defend myself. And if I were knocked unconscious, I wouldn't have a chance to tell you why I'm here."

"Then tell me why you're here and I'll decide afterward whether you're worth taking a punch at."

"I'm here to offer you a job," Franco said, breathing an audible sigh of relief. "Basic security. What you're good at. No, let me rephrase that. What you're the best at."

"No way. I think it's time for me to retire from the security business. I've done enough damage. I think I'll take up something less controversial—like dog grooming or house-sitting."

Dylan slumped into the porch swing. The prince took the wicker chair across from him. He wiped the rain from his forehead with a handkerchief.

"I think you might be useful to us."

"That's exactly what Cuthbert thought. And I guess he was right, wasn't he?"

"Mr. MacPhail, I told you I'm here to offer you a job. But I'm also here to offer you an apology."

"An apology?"

"Yes. Lord Cuthbert used you, because he wanted to trap Serena. He used her weakness—her desire to give love and be loved. Cuthbert thought he was helping me but he didn't know that I've changed—so much so that I don't need or want his kind of help."

"Changed?"

"Yes. I used to be an unhappy man. I was required to marry by our constitution. I was required to marry a woman who is perfectly beautiful and gracious and loving and kind—but isn't the woman I love. I spent many years being quite bitter about that. But now I'm happy. Happy with Lady Jane Howard, the woman I love.''

Dylan gave him a sullen stare. ''I'm glad one of us is happy.''

''I don't mean that as any sort of boast,'' the prince said. ''I only meant it as an explanation for why I am offering you this job. I can see people more clearly, understand them better, and allow them the freedom to be different from me. All because I see things through the lens of happiness.''

''I'm thrilled for you,'' Dylan said dryly. ''Does that mean you've reconsidered exiling Serena to the Isle of Whit?''

''That was a plan drawn up by my advisers,'' Franco admitted. ''I regret it very much. I will not require her to go, and in fact, I have appointed her to another position within the monarchy.''

''And what's this job you're offering me?''

''I want you to provide security for my two sons. They are determined to go to Northwestern University here in Chicago.''

''And what's the secret catch?''

''There is none.''

''You know my record. You know what happened. Twice I've been used. Twice I've failed the one person I thought I would protect.''

''I know. And many other times you succeeded. I want to hire you. I have two children who keep telling me that Northwestern is a great football school—and that they'll do some learning. They need security.''

"Well, forget it. You can get anybody to do that kind of thing. Get off my porch. I've decided not to punch you, and I'd suggest you leave before I reconsider.''

"All right, I'm going, but I hope you change your mind. About the job, not the punch.''

Prince Franco stood and seemed to turn to go. But then he reached out and touched the envelope of pictures, tugging on one picture's border so that its image was visible.

Dylan set his jaw tight, ready to fight for possession of them.

"I won't ask you how you got these,'' the prince said. "But I will simply say I admire you. I am convinced you are, quite simply, the best at what you do. And I am hopeful you will reconsider my job offer.''

"Got anything else you want to say before you get out of here?''

"Yes. The president says to tell your mother that he shall dine with her tomorrow evening.''

Dylan glowered.

"He gave you quite a glowing job recommendation,'' the prince concluded. "Good night.''

Dylan grunted. He watched the prince saunter to the waiting limousine.

"Jerk,'' he said under his breath. And then he felt a catch in his throat.

From behind the door of the sleek limousine, he saw a grass-stained sneaker touch the street—followed by a long, blue-jeaned leg.

"Hey, Prince!"

"Yes, Mr. MacPhail?"

"How much are you paying?"

The prince named a sum.

"I'll give it some thought. I'll get back to you."

"Thank you, Mr. MacPhail."

And, with a friendly goodbye to Serena, Prince Franco got into the limousine.

Serena walked up to the bottom porch step.

"You got your hair cut," she observed.

"Yeah, well, it was getting in my eyes."

"Looks nice. I betcha half the men in the world are going to get their locks chopped off next week."

"Not likely."

She glanced over her shoulder. "Do I send them on their way or do I tell them to wait for me?"

"Depends on what you're here for," he said.

"To offer my own apology. For not giving you the benefit of the doubt. For believing what others told me. For being so scared for myself and my sons that I didn't think about the fact that you're an honorable man."

"And? Any other reasons for being here?"

"Just this."

Trotting up the steps, she flung her arms around him, drawing him into a long, sweet kiss.

"Tell that driver to go home," Dylan said.

They looked back at the empty curb.

"I guess he already has," Serena said. She glanced over at the wicker table. "Oh, my God, where did you get these?"

"Princess, it's not what you think."

"You don't know what I think. Tell me how you got the pictures…and what you were going to do with them?"

"I stole them from Cuthbert."

"How did you ever manage?"

"That, my dear, is my secret," he said, reaching down and gathering the pictures—and negatives—in a single swipe. "And as for what I was going to do with them…"

He opened the screen door and escorted her into the warm living room. Firelight danced on the ceiling. The logs hissed and sputtered.

"This, my Princess, is what I was going to do with them," he said.

He flung the pictures and negatives into the fireplace. There was a sharp protest by the logs, a whistling sound and then the pictures browned and curled at the corners. Within minutes, there was nothing left. Nothing left at all of their indiscretion.

"I'd never betray you. I've never told another woman that I loved her. Because I never loved before. Until I met you. I love you, Serena. Even if you walk out that door and never come back to me, I will still love you."

Serena took a deep breath.

"But you know I can't see you again," she said.
The devastation on his face was quick and sure.
"What?"

She added quickly, "I love you. But how would it look for the dowager princess to date her sons' bodyguard?"

A wicked smile stole across his features. "We don't have to date," he said, drawing her into his embrace. "We had a very long first date. We don't need a second one. I got another idea."

"I'm sure you do," Serena said. "After all, you are the best."

And they came together with a kiss as white-hot as the fire crackling in the fireplace.

Epilogue

Far away, in a run-down castle on the Isle of Whit, a sixteen-inch television flickered on. In the darkened room, the old man, his bulbous nose pink with cold, stared mournfully at the screen. He tugged the blanket up around his shoulders, shivering against the draft. The helicopter had just left, the pilot telling him that it seemed to be an exceptionally early winter and that he wouldn't be coming back much before spring.

"This is 'Entertainment Tonight.' Prince Franco attended a very special, very quiet wedding ceremony in Chicago today. The former Princess Serena married private security expert Dylan MacPhail in the Wrigleyville neighborhood church he attended as a child."

The man reached into his sweater pocket for a tin of peppermints. He glared at the image of the elegant woman in a white knee-length shift. The dashing fellow in a tuxedo had his arm around her waist.

"Rumors are flying that while the former Princess

has maintained her slender figure, she will soon be ready to announce that she and MacPhail will become parents."

The man rubbed the bridge of his nose. Six months later, it still hurt. He had never figured out why a maid at the Drake punched him. The police had been no help whatsoever, and Officer Kerner, who had so solemnly and attentively listened to Cuthbert's theories on law enforcement, had laughed uproariously when the Lord of the Chamber reported the assault to him.

As long as he lived, Cuthbert would never understand Americans.

"The radiant bride wore her signature close-cropped hairdo and her two sons, young heartthrobs Prince Erik and Prince Vlad jointly served as best man. Prince Erik attends Northwestern University as an undergraduate business major while Prince Vlad is preparing to attend the university's computer science department. The groom's sister Charlotte MacPhail, a detective in the Chicago Police Department, was the maid of honor and caught the white rose bouquet from the bride. After the private ceremony, guests were treated to chicken-fried steak and mashed potatoes at the home of Serena's new mother-in-law...."

The old man rose in his seat. There was something familiar about Serena's new mother-in-law, a fifty-something woman in the lemon yellow print suit.

Something so oddly familiar…made him think of a pink maid's uniform.

Suddenly, he knew.

"Shut that bloody thing off!" Lord Cuthbert bellowed.

Take 4 bestselling love stories FREE

Plus get a FREE surprise gift!

Where were you when the storm blew in?

Snowbound

Three stormy stories about what happens to three snowbound couples, from three of your favorite authors:

SHOTGUN WEDDING by Charlotte Lamb
MURDER BY THE BOOK by Margaret St. George
ON A WING AND A PRAYER by Jackie Weger

Find out if cabin fever can melt the snow this December!

Available wherever Harlequin and Silhouette books are sold.

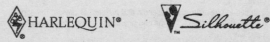

HARLEQUIN®   Silhouette®

As Seen on TV!

Free Gift Offer

With a Free Gift proof-of-purchase
from any Harlequin® book, you can receive
a beautiful cubic zirconia pendant.

This stunning marquise-shaped stone is a genuine cubic
zirconia—accented by an 18" gold tone necklace.
(Approximate retail value $19.95)

Send for yours today...
compliments of ◈HARLEQUIN®

To receive your free gift, a cubic zirconia pendant, send us one original proof-of-purchase, photocopies not accepted, from the back of any Harlequin Romance®, Harlequin Presents®, Harlequin Temptation®, Harlequin Superromance®, Harlequin Love & Laughter®, Harlequin Intrigue®, Harlequin American Romance®, or Harlequin Historicals® title available at your favorite retail outlet, together with the Free Gift Certificate, plus a check or money order for $1.65 u.s./$2.15 CAN. (do not send cash) to cover postage and handling, payable to Harlequin Free Gift Offer. We will send you the specified gift. Allow 6 to 8 weeks for delivery. Offer good until March 31, 1998, or while quantities last. Offer valid in the U.S. and Canada only.

Free Gift Certificate

Name: _____

Address: _____

City: _____ State/Province: _____ Zip/Postal Code: _____

Mail this certificate, one proof-of-purchase and a check or money order for postage and handling to: HARLEQUIN FREE GIFT OFFER 1998. In the U.S.: 3010 Walden Avenue, P.O. Box 9071, Buffalo NY 14269-9057. In Canada: P.O. Box 604, Fort Erie, Ontario L2Z 5X3.

FREE GIFT OFFER   084-KEZ
ONE PROOF-OF-PURCHASE
To collect your fabulous FREE GIFT, a cubic zirconia pendant, you must include this
original proof-of-purchase for each gift with the properly completed Free Gift Certificate.

084-KEZR2

KEY TO MY HEART

Unlock the secrets of romance just in time for the most romantic day of the year—Valentine's Day!

Key to My Heart
features three of your favorite authors,

Kasey Michaels,
Rebecca York
and Muriel Jensen,

to bring you wonderful tales of romance and Valentine's Day dreams come true.

As an added bonus you can receive Harlequin's special Valentine's Day necklace. FREE with the purchase of every *Key to My Heart* collection.

Available in January,
wherever Harlequin books are sold.

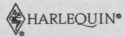

HARLEQUIN®

PHKEY349